The B Gene II

The Rise of Akache

By
Carlos Hardy

The B Gene II

Dedication

Thank you for supporting the second book in the B-Gene series. It is with great humility and pleasure that I present this book to you. I would like to give a special thanks to my amazing book Editor Victoria Sacino for such easy and fun edit sessions. Also I would like to shout out Sunny Chayes, my official proofer for reading every book I've written, while offering sound advice on story development. I really hope you enjoy the progression of the story. Happy Reading.

Email: info@carloshardy.com

Chapter 1
The Pods Are Coming!

A clear nighttime sky; pitch-dark against a multitude of bright stars twinkling with promise. What a mesmerizing backdrop for such a chaotic night. Miniature Akache modtron pods – hundreds of them – glide across the star-studded sky, each leaving behind a trail of red smoke. This is the signal to the beginning of the Akache war against the United States of America.

In the past few hours leading up to this event, the eyes of nearly every American have been glued to their television screens. Some terrified, some intrigued as they watch the unknown ships currently taking over the airspace in Washington, D.C. Military jets keep the Akache pods at bay, maintaining a barely comfortable divide between the two sides. The pods hover, waiting for the precise moment to strike.

Beneath the pending war in the sky, Caleb and Jaylen rush toward the Lincoln Memorial Reflecting Pool. The teen boys leap into the chilly waters, sloshing wildly as they make it to the other side. They emerge from the pool and race for the National Mall.

Jaylen reaches out and grabs Caleb by the shirt. "Bro, wait, this is silly." Caleb stops in his tracks. "What are you saying? How can you and this alien bastard be one and the same?"

Caleb yanks his shirt free from Jaylen's grip. He finds it curious that Jaylen wants to have this conversation right now — but obliges. "I can't explain it, Jaylen, but you have to trust me. We don't have a lot of time to stop them."

"Are you fucking out of your mind?! What has America done for us, bro? It undoubtedly would serve America right if these alien bastards got the upper hand."

"I can't explain how, but things aren't always what they seem," Caleb replies. "I feel it."

Jaylen steps right into Caleb's personal space with an icy look in his eyes, determined to win this one. "Haven't you been paying attention, Cal? Those things in that ship are huge, strong, and indestructible. We don't stand a chance. Bro, they have no limits. And for once, someone is helping out the Black cause. You said it yourself — they're not after us. White people! I say fuck it; we fight with Akache."

No amount of Jaylen's reasoning has an impact on Caleb. He tries to keep quiet, but he can't resist. "Jaylen, you don't understand.

Our civilization depends on us doing the right thing."

Jaylen rolls his eyes and shakes his head before looking skyward. "Caleb, for the first time in our lifetime we've got a shot at evening the score. It looks like they have a date with 'White America,' and that doesn't involve us." Jaylen paces. If only it were as easy to convince Caleb as when they were kids working up the courage to steal candy from the corner store.

Caleb sits down on a nearby cement ledge, mulling over Jaylen's words. "But what if you are wrong, Jaylen?"

"Negro, I'm not wrong. I say we stay out of it – but watch from afar," Jaylen adds, with a gleeful smirk.

A stabbing pain suddenly pierces Caleb in the center of his chest. His face twists in agony. "Fuck! Ahhhhh, God… What is that?!"

Jaylen races to Caleb's side, placing a comforting hand on his shoulder. "Caleb, what is it?" Time seems to stop as Jaylen watches Caleb's eyes roll back into his head, pupils dilated. Caleb tries but fails at shaking off the fast-encroaching haze. With stern conviction in his voice, he begins chanting uncontrollably, a garbled mess.

Jaylen watches in shock, unfamiliar with the language spewing from Caleb's mouth.

Hoping to bring him out of it, Jaylen lands a gentle slap on Caleb's face. "Yo, Caleb, bro, what's wrong? Snap out of it."

Caleb shakes his head, his mind drifting back to reality. His demeanor quickly morphs from calm to frantic, and he rises to his feet. "We got to go." He grabs Jaylen's arm. They take off running toward the White House.

A few minutes later, the teens reach Pennsylvania Avenue, uneasily glancing over their shoulders. They brace for what may soon arise out of the darkness enveloping the sky. They peer upward, tracking the swarm of pod ships as they inch ever closer and closer to the White House. Doing their best to keep out of the enemy's sight, the boys weave in and out between the trees that line the avenue.

Tourists flood the surrounding street corners, protesting the onslaught of hovering pods with various obscenities. "This is America! Go home," one of them shouts. "We don't want you here," adds another. Meanwhile, other tourists keep a low profile, sneaking videos for social media on their phone. Obnoxious reporters congregate on both sides of the streets. Each one does their own live broadcast, hoping to secure footage of a response from the invaders.

Caleb and Jaylen fight their way through the crowd, pushing past several rowdy bystanders until they emerge near the front gate leading to the White House. Blocking the entrance is a human wall made of big, hulking military soldiers, each draped in all-encompassing riot gear. Guns drawn, fingers glued to the trigger. They are clearly not fucking around, and Jaylen knows it.

"So, what's the plan now, Caleb?"

"We have to get to the President."

Jaylen sends an icy glare to the barrier of soldiers up ahead. "Bro, they will shoot us like we stole something. They are about that life. I just want to watch this shit go down on their dime."

"Jaylen, keep quiet. You clearly can't see past the hatred that has been indoctrinated within."

Jaylen's voice rises with rage. He accusingly points at the sky. "Bro, I didn't bring them here! The chickens have come home to roost. Facts."

Caleb takes in Jaylen's impassioned explosion for just a moment — before returning his attention to the White House, his eyes nearly boring into the bodies of the soldiers. "We have to warn them." He evades his friend's judging eyes and steps out from behind the tree he's been shielding himself with. Caleb stands directly in front of the boisterous crowd, skimming the radius from where he stands in relation to the front entrance of the White House. Jaylen reluctantly joins him. Caleb points. "That's where we have to go."

"And how are we supposed to get there?"

"Peacefully."

"Caleb, I think you were on that ship too long, bro. You are losing your grip on reality. Storming the White House would get us killed without question."

Caleb ignores the harsh warning and pushes his way through the crowd, soon closing in on the heavily guarded entrance. He shakes with trepidation. As the brisk night drains the warmth from his body, the tip of his nose turns bright red and his teeth chatter uncontrollably. He steps up to the Commanding General, with Jaylen lagging behind. "I need to see the President."

A white guard, with squared shoulders and a shaved head, marches over to the boys. "You don't belong here." There is complete silence as the guard maintains his intensity, with one eye on Caleb and the other on the Akache pods overhead. "Go on, kid. Get away from here."

"But you don't understand. I can help. I need to see the President."

In unison, the surrounding soldiers hoist up their guns, aiming at the two boys. Caleb's lips kiss the barrel of the nearest gun.

The white guard stares down at him. "Get away from here."

Terrified on the inside, Caleb steals a whiff of metallic emanating from the weapon staring him in the face — but he doesn't budge. Jaylen's arms are reaching for the sky. He's nearly frozen with fear and speaks in a slow, careful manner. "I am going to put my hands to my side, officer. Don't shoot."

Suddenly, a penetrating vibration rattles the Earth beneath their feet, shifting everyone within a mile from side to side. The soldiers lift their weapons, locking in on the pods in the sky.

"It's them! It's the alien scum," the Commanding General shouts, spewing each word with pure hatred.

Caleb closes his eyes for a moment, centering himself. His shoulders relax. Confidence swells within him, taking charge and eclipsing his fear. Time seems to stop as he takes a calculated step forward. The powerful stride of Caleb's step forcefully pushes each soldier back a few inches, their boots uncontrollably skidding across the gravel. Several loud gasps echo through the crowd. All eyes are on Caleb now. The teen takes another guided step, and the entire brigade of soldiers splits in half, each one getting pushed toward either side of the street. The crowd watches. Some cower on the ground, praying for mercy, while the shock of others' quickly turns to fear. Jaylen stares in awe at the unearthly scene – a tale seemingly straight out of the Book of Moses, complete with the powerful parting of the Red Sea; but in this case, soldiers. Paralyzed, the soldiers are helpless as they watch the boys make their escape.

With no time to waste, they push open the metal gate and scurry up the grand U-shaped driveway.

"How did you do that, Caleb?" Jaylen asks.

"I don't know… It just happened."

Soon, their size thirteens land at the threshold leading into the White House. A sense of blistering heat snakes its way up Caleb's spine and settles on the back of his neck. He swings around to find the alien pods hovering over the houses of innocent citizens. Caleb sidelines his nerves and forces his open palm into the sky as a symbol of peace.

Jaylen smacks him on the back, jerking him back to reality. "What the fuck are you doing?"

"I'm trying to save lives."

"Bro, we gotta talk. This shit is getting way weird. We jumping out of ships, you hurling cars at people, your eyes closing every five damn minutes..." Caleb's eyes flutter before closing again. "What now?"

"Shhh... I feel them." Caleb wobbles on his feet, his legs shifting from the left to the right, over and over. He no longer has control of his body. "It's too strong..." His feet slowly lift off the ground.

Jaylen notices. "Bro. Bro. Caleb, what's happening?"

The double doors leading to the White House abruptly spring open. A glaring white light blinds them for a few moments. They use their forearms to shield their eyes, unable to see what's coming. A rapid-fire zap of electricity jolts through their bodies, sending them to the ground hard. They flail about violently, attempting to fight the debilitating pain and at least remain conscious — but it's too much. The boys' excruciating cries flood into the atmosphere and away with the cold, chaotic night. They finally settle down — silent, motionless, and unconscious. A few

Secret Service agents emerge from the White House and surround them, their guns drawn.

Caleb and Jaylen each lie on a cold metal lab table. Caleb's shirt has been ripped from his back. A single lightbulb dangles overhead, softly illuminating the space. Metal cuffs bind the teens' hands to the tables, restricting movement. The two drift in and out of consciousness.

Hushed voices tickle Caleb's eardrums as he struggles to make out words. Cold hands trace the intricate designs on his back, which have grown even more colorful and pronounced.

A disembodied voice cuts through the silence, and the unknown man glides through the shadows, stopping right next to Caleb's unconscious form.

"These are not self-inflicted," one Secret Service agent comments. "They are a part of his DNA."

The unknown man steps out from the darkness. It's Mark Fitz from Science and Technology. "This may be the missing piece of the puzzle."

"He's only about sixteen, maybe seventeen," another agent says.

Fitz turns toward the agents and shoots them a disapproving glare. The agents take the hint and retreat to the back of the room. Fitz gently traces his fingertips along the designs on Caleb's back. He gleefully murmurs into a small recorder. "These designs are magnificent. Similar to the ones from the ship in my warehouse. They are indeed our gateway. A language all of its own. Both assailants breached White House security. My guess… The elaborate designs are where the power lives."

Suddenly Caleb's metal lab table trembles. His body vibrates uncontrollably. The agents cautiously step into the light, their guns drawn.

"Shoot!!"

Chapter 2
Whose Side Are THEY On?

"Hold your fire." From out of the darkness, a husky voice intervenes. All gunfire halts as President Reid steps into the light, his pale face riddled with wrinkles, his underwhelming smirk reeking of uncertainty. The President sidles up next to Caleb, who still lies unresponsive on the metal lab table. His eyebrows raise curiously as he examines the markings on Caleb's back. The surprised look on the President's face makes it clear he's never seen anything like this — but he reserves his judgment. "Who is he? What is he?"

The President's Aide nervously takes a step forward, a classified file in hand. "Caleb Prescott, sixteen, from the outskirts of Washington. HBCU freshman. Mother passed years ago. His father lives north of here." He closes the folder and retreats back to the darkness.

President Reid's eyes stay locked in on Caleb's back, mesmerized by the vibrant sketching. "I've never seen anything like this... Is it a language?"

On the opposite side of the table, Fitz is in investigation mode, excitedly admiring the iridescent pattern. His shaggy reddish locks flop in his face, but he allows nothing to break his concentration.

His joyous demeanor seems out of place, and the President watches, puzzled. "What do you think it is? A map?"

Fitz welcomes the unsolicited questions and replies proudly, as if speaking to a group of cadets at one of his Science and Technology conventions. "These writings are meaningful only for the purpose of life, unknown to us. These designs, I'm sure, have created worlds beyond our knowing. The images are similar to the ones found on the ship where I work." President Reid hovers over Fitz's shoulder, literally breathing down his neck. Fitz gives an elated half-smile to no one in particular as his fingertips graze over the unusual patterns. A blistering red steam rises up from the markings, forcing back the kooky scientist's hand. "Whoa, that's hot. That's very interesting and purposed…" His eyes widen, intrigue pushing him to resume despite the risk. He revels in the mere possibility of conquering the unknown. The searing heat emanating from Caleb's back fails to deter him. Instead, he becomes even more fixated on nabbing a sample of the specimen. With his hand, Fitz caresses each line making up the delicate pattern.

President Reid's booming voice cuts through the awkward moment. "Mark, enough!"

"You don't understand, Mr. President." Eyes still glued to the markings, Fitz stumbles over words as he rushes to his own defense. "We can conduct experiments that could lead to profound remedies in our medicine, and I'm hopeful our longevity as humans can be extended based on research. There is something here. It's waiting for us to conquer it… Explore it. It's how science shows itself to us, Mr. President."

The President turns to his Aide and nods, prompting him to exit the room. Then it's just the two of them – President Reid and Fitz. President Reid again examines the discoloration on Caleb's body. "He's not a fucking alien, Mark," he says, choosing his words carefully. "He's an American. He's one of us."

Fitz silently concedes, all the while still entranced by the designs, not allowing them to escape his sight even for a moment. He folds his arms across his chest. "I just need one vial of blood from him," Fitz says, desperately pushing his own agenda on White House grounds, a clear breach of protocol.

"We can't do that, Mark."

"Mr. President, that single vial of blood can be a matter of life or death for all of us. I suggest you make an executive decision right now."

President Reid considers Fitz's words, turning back to Caleb's lifeless body. "Okay, one vial."

Not a second later, the giddy scientist produces a small plastic syringe from his lab coat pocket. He extracts a single vial of blood from Caleb's arm. A door at the back of the room is suddenly flung open. Fitz hastily shoves the syringe into his pocket and ducks out of the room just as Homeland Security Advisor Brad Doley enters. President Reid looks up. Beads of sweat pour down Doley's crumpled forehead. Sweat stains form under his armpits. Quickly, the President pulls him aside.

"What do you know, Doley?"

"We need to talk privately."

"This room is secure. This is about as private as it's going to get."

Doley nervously eyes the single hanging lightbulb in the center of the room. He shifts closer to the President. "We counted seven hundred and fifty pods, ships, foreign objects, whatever you want to call them," he whispers.

"How close are they?"

Doley rubs the back of his balding head, hesitating, pleading with himself not to withhold information. Then again, he's never been good at censoring himself, so he continues. "The ships have been at a standstill for the last few hours. The military is on high alert and ready at your command. Our intelligence agencies can't seem to break through their robust technology. It's rock solid, Mr. President."

President Reid's confidence plummets. He pulls Doley closer. "Was the Melanin Experiment a mistake?"

"Look, we gave them what they wanted – one million of our own – and it looks like they are going to fuck us with no lube. Not even a kiss on the forehead." Doley looks past the President's shoulder at Caleb, still unconscious. Soon, he manages to gather his train of thought, despite the dire circumstances.

President Reid scans the darkness, his eyes desperate, searching for a way to process what's happening. "How about Europe?"

"Nothing, Mr. President. Looks like we remain more popular. Besides, who really gives a fuck about Europe?" A disapproving frown from the President urges Doley to relinquish his alarming bias and rhetoric.

"Doley, what about Japan? China? Africa?"

"We are on our own, Mr. President. The United States seems to have won the raffle." Doley inches closer, his protruding belly nearly kissing the President's belt. "One other thing. We are certain that something's holding them back from striking."

"Holding them back? What are you talking about, Doley?"

With one final step closer, the scent of Doley's coffee breath swirls just beneath the President's nostrils. "They've had every opportunity to strike our military, but they haven't. Why?"

President Reid runs his fingers through his thick hair, taking a deep breath and trying to maintain a sense of reality.

"I'm sorry, Mr. President, but the Melanin Experiment is a failed policy. They will strike. Convincing every Black American to join our side will probably take an act of God."

"How much time do we have?"

"I'm not certain. Maybe a few hours…" Doley looks over just in time to see Caleb regaining consciousness. He rests a curious hand on his chin for a moment. He removes his glasses and blows a few puffs of breath to clean them before returning them to their position. He dispels an inner sense of angst from the back of his throat. He turns his focus back to the President. "Mr. President, the last time this room was used was in 1947 – Roswell. I should know the truth. Is this kid what they are after? Is he one of them?"

"No. I don't know, Doley. We are hoping he can provide some insight."

"And if he can't?"

President Reid takes in Doley's harrowing words. Suddenly, he approaches the door and exits the room. Doley sprints after him. The two men reach the elevators, where two Secret Service agents hold the doors apart. The President slips inside the confines of the quaint space. "You coming? We can talk more upstairs."

Doley combs his mind for a proper response, one measured with precision. "I'll meet you upstairs. I left my clipboard back in the room." President Reid nods and the agents allow the elevator doors to close. Doley turns to face the room where Caleb is being held captive. He stares at the door uncomfortably. He reenters.

The distinguished advisor removes his coat jacket and stuffs it under his armpit. Now, he's all business. He nudges Caleb with his forearm. "Wake up," Doley says, in a gruff tone.

Caleb's eyes slowly open. A relaxed sense of confidence oozes from his pores. "I wasn't sleeping."

"What do you know about them?"

"I know as much as you do."

"Don't get smart with me, boy." Doley's nostrils flare in anger. He clenches his fist.

Caleb rolls over on the metal lab table, trying to catch a glimpse of Doley's face. "I've seen you on television, Advisor Doley. You assisted with the Melanin Experiment, displacing one million innocent Black people. You gave THEM the ammunition, and now they will use it against you."

"What are you talking about?" Doley snaps. Caleb maintains his calm demeanor, unaffected, unblinking. "Look, I'm asking the questions here."

"Are you? Or are you searching for answers that will never come?"

Doley grows increasingly enraged, wrapping his meaty hand around Caleb's neck. Caleb struggles to break free from the grip. "You'll talk now, asshole. What do you know?" Doley screams in Caleb's face.

"I know as much as you do," Caleb replies.

Doley's hand squeezes even tighter, his rage creeping into his grip. He's not letting go.

"What do you fucking know, boy? Who are they?"

All of a sudden Caleb's body contorts, sliding back and forth across the table. His uncontrollably fuming emotions somehow provide him with strength and stamina. He inhales Doley's vicious tropes, which mysteriously seem to invigorate his entire being. Caleb's hand lifts, violently striking Doley in the chest with such force that it sends him clear across the darkened room.

After catching his breath, Doley wipes the dust from his uniform and rises to his feet. He hesitates, barely certain that what he just witnessed was in fact real. "You are one of them. You are one of them."

"No, I am not."

Doley cowers nearby, silently watching as Caleb breaks free from his metal cuffs.

Chapter 3
Let Us Go

A shirtless Caleb nonchalantly tosses aside the metal cuffs that were holding him hostage on the frigid lab table. Doley gets a shocking eyeful of Caleb's newfound dominance.

Amid all of the commotion, Jaylen finally starts to come around. He rolls over, gently rubbing the back of his neck. "What happened? Did I hit my head? Those bastards."

Doley shifts his attention to Jaylen, quickly scouring his body for any trace of designs similar to the ones on Caleb's back. "Are you one of them?"

The cuffs around Jaylen's wrists halt his escape as he tries to roll off the table. "What is this fool talking about, Cal?"

Caleb steps closer to his friend. He pops the lock on the cuffs and frees Jaylen. "He thinks we're Akache," Caleb explains.

Jaylen takes in a full 360 of the small enclosed room. "Where are we?" He rubs the sleep from his eyes, suspiciously focusing in on Doley, who stares right back.

"How did you two get here?" Doley asks, taking a few methodical steps back. "Ship? Pod?"

Caleb raises his arms skyward. He tries reasoning with the inquisitive advisor. "Look, we have no weapons. They will not stop until they kill every white American."

Jaylen places a concerned hand on Caleb's chest. "I say who cares! Fuck it! America don't care about us. Why should we care about them?"

"Please, Jaylen, you'll make things worse."

"These mofos never had our best interest! Why should we have theirs?!" Jaylen's boisterous tone climbs. Caleb opens his mouth to speak, hoping to calm down his friend — but Jaylen keeps it up. "Naw, Cal. I say we play this shit out. It's survival of the fittest." Standing off to the side, trying to remain silent, Doley soaks up every last drop of information the boys dare to give.

"I need to warn the President," Caleb insists. "The Akache alliance is powerful, and we don't have much time."

Doley finally pipes up, contemplating Caleb's warning. "How powerful are they?"

"You wouldn't understand. We are wasting time."

A coaxing grin on Jaylen's face catches Doley's eye. "Cal, are you defending these douchebags, bro? After slavery, Jim Crow, police brutality… I say let the war commence."

"I'd rather defend humanity, Jaylen. Without it, we got nothing."

"No!" Jaylen pushes Caleb back, a mixture of anger and betrayal on his face. "We got an army out there, ready to defend us, BRO." He paces the room, faster and faster, his adrenaline taking over, pumping through his body. He roughly punches a fist into his palm for good measure. "They'll come fast and hard, bro. America's fucking little military will have no chance." He turns to Doley. "I've seen them in action, Mr. White Collar — they're no joke. This shit is gonna hit the fan, and I'm here for it." Studying Doley's face, Jaylen silently wishes he'd crack or at least give them a fighting chance to make a run for it.

Doley shifts his weight hesitantly, searching for the proper rebuttal. "Okay, you've said your piece, and now I will say mine. One million Black Americans chose to enter the lottery. That's what they wanted."

Jaylen shoves an accusing finger in Doley's direction, his throat tight. "You rat-faced liar! You offered those families a small stipend that would last a week, bro. America deserves what it gets."

The hairs on the back of Doley's neck stand up. His inner rage boils over. "The government had a vested interest to protect all Americans. All lives matter—"

Jaylen cuts off the advisor, disgusted. "The funny thing is, y'all actually believe that shit. Like Malcolm said, 'By any means necessary,' bro," Jaylen says with a closed fist held high in the air, signifying his allegiance to the Black to Black Movement. "He didn't say the 'bro' part, but you know what I mean, White Collar."

Going nowhere fast with Jaylen, Doley shifts his focus to Caleb, who comes across as the more reasonable one of the two. "How do we stop them?"

"That's a question I can't answer, Doley," Caleb cooly replies.

"Answer me!" Doley's tone grows ever harsher — he's completely forgone his golden rule of remaining calm amid interrogations. "How do we stop them?!"

Jaylen makes a fast move, instantly up in Doley's face. "You are a crook. You want us to help you but you shit all over our communities. Get the hell outta here." He pushes back slightly for emphasis.

Shoving his hands in his pockets, Doley takes a moment to contemplate before making the wrong move. He inches closer to the boys.

"Let's be honest, fellas. They are outnumbered. I'm sure you both know what I mean. The United States will defeat you if you are with them — that, I will promise."

Caleb swiftly turns his back to the advisor, his controlled words exuding purpose. "The strength of the Akache extends beyond what is in front of you. They have waited thousands of years to find what they are looking for, and it has led them here. They won't let up until they have recolonized." Suddenly, Caleb thuds against the table, his shoulders slumped. His eyes droop toward the floor. Both Doley and Jaylen wait with bated breath for more details of this daunting prognosis.

The following words cut through the silence like a hot knife slashing through cold butter. "I feel something inside of me. It's stronger than I could have imagined. It won't let me go, pulling at the worst part of me. I think it wants to destroy me, Jaylen." Caleb steels himself, the controlled speech pattern returns, once more spewing revelations from deep within his soul. "Karnitu, their leader, is a tyrant, and he'll stop at nothing—" Caleb doubles over, clutching at his chest. He releases a horrifying scream.

Jaylen rushes over to help his friend, forcing him back onto the metal lab table.

"Cal, what is it? Bro, are you okay? Stop that shit!"

"It's trying to kill me. It wants to kill me!"

"Who?? What?!" Jaylen pleads.

Caleb's eyes well up. He curls into a ball, trying to fight the pain. A darker tone gradually obscures the hue of his bronzed skin. "It wants to kill me."

"Bro, you are talking real crazy. You see what these governmental hacks have done to you??" Jaylen spins on his heels, screaming to no one. "Yo, what y'all do to him?!"

Doley's heard about all he can stand. He heartlessly veers past Jaylen. "You'll be dead by morning," he growls before slamming the door shut behind him. Caleb suddenly drops from the lab table. His body mysteriously slides from one end of the room to the other. He's terrified, flailing about, trying to stop the motion. Finally, Caleb's body settles in an adjacent corner of the room. Baffled, yet concerned, Jaylen stares, frozen in place. He watches as Caleb's breathing calms and his strength wanes.

Tears form under Caleb's eyelids, but he holds them in tight — he's too afraid; afraid to move, even to simply shed his tears. "Jaylen, I don't want to die." Jaylen forces himself to choke back his emotions. Instead, he clenches his teeth and buries his reddening face in the shadows. Between the two boys, Caleb has always been the pinnacle of strength, the one who never gave up, no matter the circumstances. Forced to watch his best friend suffer from such agony, Jaylen's barely keeping it together… It's killing him on the inside.

Without any warning, Jaylen manages to muster up some strength and sprints to the door. His most prominent emotion now is rage. He pounds on the door relentlessly. "Let us out!! Let us out of here!!"

Having ascended from the secret underground exam room, just one mile underneath the White House, Doley waits as the elevator doors open. He steps out, gladly hogging as much fresh air as he can fit into his lungs. The White House's corridor overflows with generals and other military personnel rushing about as they scramble to prepare the United States for the impending war with the Akache invaders. Hundreds of soldiers patrol the various secret halls within.

Two Secret Service agents flank Doley, escorting him through the building. Both agents are armed with weapons, the bulging outlines of which are casually obscured beneath their suit jackets. The agents silently lead Doley to the Situation Room. Upon reaching their destination, one of the agents scans his security placard against the door's identification interface, gaining access to the room. The door audibly unlocks and creaks open.

Doley enters the secure room, his mind seemingly elsewhere. Caleb's revelations incessantly replay in his head. So far, he's been unable to shake them. Cabinet members and top generals fill the room.

President Reid turns to everyone, wearing a nervous smirk. He attempts to clear away a lump in his throat. "Are we all set, gentlemen?"

Doley's presence goes unnoticed as he slithers into a chair at the very back of the room. He surveys everyone there – the only people present are white men. Although he's never noticed this fact in the past, today its painfully obvious.

A top general with a country-like twang heads the impromptu meeting. "Gentlemen. The geographical landscape of these pods are strategically positioned, making it extremely difficult for our military to garner leverage– "

"How many more pods are there?" President Reid interrupts.

"Too many to count, Mr. President." A sobering hush falls across the room as each

Cabinet member comes to terms with the unnerving news they've been given.

All at once each of the ten televisions across the room switch on. Chilling images featuring the horde of Akache pods fill the screens. The video footage shows the pods hovering over many populated, predominantly white, cities. On the city streets, a determined group of Americans parade around, demanding attention from the galactic ships. Some mindlessly scream obscenities to the sky, while others remain peaceful, holding signs to welcome the invaders.

The general resumes his intelligence briefing, everyone entranced by the footage showing on the television. "In practically every one of our cities, we are outmatched by these ships. The specifics of what they want have been administered." Doley swallows hard and squeezes the arm of his chair, wishing for his jitters to magically subside. The general turns to the Cabinet members with a serious look on his face. "These ships are specifically targeting white American suburbs."

"How sure are we about that?" the President asks with concern in his voice.

"I wish I could provide an alternative outcome, but the intelligence is real, Mr.

President." All eyes shift to President Reid, waiting for their next instruction.

On the televisions behind them, the distorted images of the pods suddenly fade away, morphing into the fierce Akache commander, Karnitu, who is positioned on the peak of an unknown mountain. This signal is getting broadcast to millions of televisions across America. Everyone in the room stares, eyes glued to the intriguing yet horrifying, imagery. The menacing Akache commander's face is covered in ancient markings and he has a red-colored ponytail that sits securely atop his head. His body is garment free, the muscles in his shoulders pronounced, bulging. Even more haunting is Karnitu's slanted forehead.

President Reid steps closer to one of the televisions, his eyes squinting in thought as he realizes… The patterns covering the commander's body are unusually similar to the markings he saw on Caleb's back not more than an hour ago.

On the television, Karnitu suddenly wraps his sharp claws around the neck of a lowly surrogate. The Cabinet members gasp as they watch the surrogate dangle from the commander's clutches, wildly flailing in an attempt to break free. Karnitu exploits the pained surrogate for the purpose of translating his Akache language — heavy, thick, and richly inflected — to English. "My Belivian brethren, people of melanin, you have suffered compounding defeats at the hand of the pale species for quite some time… Four hundred of your Earth years. The timeline you have embarked on has surely been a calamity of smoldering turmoil."

President Reid turns to his general. "Belivian? Who are they?"

"The origins of language have not been explored, but I think he's referring to Black Americans, Mr. President."

The voice of Karnitu's surrogate climbs with reassurance. "I am here for you. We are here for you. Belivians, we will rise and take back your lineage! I've come before you to warn you. The death of your lineage is upon us. The Palecians have strategized to rid the world of your existence."

Video footage of African Americans appear on the televisions; every last one of them willingly board the Akache ship, or so it looks.

"Akache is the only savior for the Belivian species. America's atrocities have reared its deceitful head long enough. It is now time to take a stand. I employ you to fight with us; become one with us. To our bland, dull enemies: your demise is quickly approaching. You will no longer have dominion over my people. I will set them free. Belivians, fight like you've never fought before." Karnitu's spear rises in triumph, an eerie warning to all who oppose his reign.

Suddenly, each television in the Situation Room shatters, one by one. Cabinet members yell out, shielding their eyes and quickly taking cover as countless shards of glass fly across the room.

The President looks at the concerned faces staring back at him, each one searching for answers. "God, have mercy on us."

Chapter 4
The Akache War

By now, it's late in the evening. Unexplainably violent winds have picked up across the United States. Akache's vile leader, Karnitu, has gone silent for the better part of an hour. Tensions soar higher and higher with each passing breath. The United States military is on high alert, waiting for Karnitu's first strike. Civilians throughout every part of the country take to the streets in a feeble attempt to gain intel on the invaders' plans. A large majority of Americans view the government's cruel melanin lottery rollout as dehumanizing and barbaric. Of course, there are some unwaveringly archaic citizens bent on maintaining a positive outlook on the lottery — to them, it's a "progressive" way of putting America first.

Grocery stories and gas stations swarm with vocally uninhibited people, all on a mission to secure goods for their families before all hell breaks loose. Streets all over the world overflow with protesters. Groups of evangelists scream out, self-righteously condemning anyone who hasn't "made it right" with their God. Some politely nod, but most of the passersby ignore the judgmental holier-than-thou folk, keeping it moving.

Street vendors on every corner peddle graphic t-shirts that scream, "It's the end of the world." The products sell out faster than the vendors can keep up. Then there are those citizens who choose to ignore all that's going on around them, and the ones who might as well be frozen in place, breathlessly staring up at the Akache pods as they hover above several hundred feet in the air.

In the grocery checkout line, a lively discussion breaks out between two women – a white woman and a Black woman – sparking pandemonium between the already crazed mob. The white woman cuts the line, angrily shoving her way to the very front with her 7-year-old in tow. She flags down the store manager with an obnoxious wave. The manager is already experiencing trouble of his own, brought on by the desperate, disorderly crowd. But he pushes his way through.

"We should be able to be first! Our families didn't receive the stipend from the lottery," the white woman shouts. The manager hurries over as quickly as possible, prodding the woman to return to her original spot in line. "This is an utter tragedy. My family needs this food." The woman stomps back to the front of the line.

"And our families do not? We waited patiently, and so should you," the Black woman replies. A handful of patrons cheer her on, some giving a thumbs up.

But the white woman refuses to give in. Instead, she uses her frail-looking daughter as a shield, wedging her in between her and the crowd. The shoppers in line direct a slew of harsh insults toward the woman.

"Ma'am—" the manager tiredly starts. He tries urging her back in line again.

The white woman turns on him. "You've got to be kidding me. They are trying to steal our country, and you're assisting them? Traitor!"

The manager's hands slide their way down his hips, defeated. "Ma'am, please just get back in line."

"No, go to hell! This is our country. We should be first!"

"What an entitled bitch," an unseen woman yells from the back of the line.

Finally, the white woman huffs in rage and retreats to the back, taunting the other customers as she walks by. She has a handful of her daughter's shirt gripped tightly in her fist, nearly dragging her along. As she passes, the Black woman sends a big "fuck you" grin her way.

The white woman is clearly displeased by this, and her gutsy New Jersey attitude comes out kicking. "And what do you have to say?"

"Nothing – except get yo' ass to the back of the line," the Black woman replies, satisfied. Customers in line share a hearty chuckle at the clever remark.

The white woman fumes, pointing to the sky, particles of spit flying from her mouth as she spews rage. "I was hoping when they came, they would finally rid us of you people forever."

With a calm demeanor, the Black woman steps out of her spot in line to face the white woman. "What do you mean 'you people'?"

An older white gentleman with a walker, an American flag bandanna tied around his neck, chimes in. "You heard her. They need to come take ya and let Africa deal witcha." The white woman nods along with him.

"And what is that supposed to mean?"

"Exactly what he said. This Melanin Experiment was supposed to do what our tax dollars didn't... Kick all foreigners out of our country."

"Amen, sweetheart," the gentleman agrees.

A group of younger customers band together, stepping out of line to surround the two dueling ladies. "Come on, guys, this isn't worth it. We all have a stake in this," a young white man says with trepidation.

The store manager comes over to the checkout line, this time with a bullhorn. "Everyone, settle down…"

The white woman goes over to the manager and yanks the bullhorn right out of his hand, using it to garner the attention of anyone within earshot. "The experiment failed, and we want our country back today! Take them – not us!"

Everything goes silent. Then in a matter of seconds, the customers form an angry mob, rioting against any person of color they can find along the crowded walkway.

Still maintaining her calm sense, the Black woman readies herself, now clenching her fist. She turns to the white woman. "Look, lady, you are crazy. No one took your country. It is as much ours as it is yours."

"You lie! The founders promised us, my family and my community, that we will be free and safe."

"Lady, we really gonna do this right now? We are in the middle of an invasion, and you talking about how this is your country?! Get on with that!"

The white woman stands firm, unmoving. "Like I said… You don't belong here, so do what is expected and go quietly, sweetie."

The Black woman turns on her heels, disgusted. Chatter spreads through the customers. She turns back, her eyes sweeping over the woman's pasty white, leathery exterior, then up toward the woman's cherry red cheeks and the irritating square-framed glasses that are too small for her face. The mere sight of her awakens an urgent sense of rage. She catches her anger before it's too late, though, counting down softly — a mental antidote to help keep her cool. "10, 9, 8, 7…" The Black woman settles as she counts to herself in the midst of the increasingly chaotic crowd. She meditates over Karnitu's infamous assertions and proclamations, his unsettling words bubble over in her mind…

The death of your lineage is upon us. The Palecians have strategized to rid the world of your existence. Akache is the only savior for the Belivian species. America's atrocities have reared its deceitful head long enough. It is now time to take a stand. I employ you to fight with us; become one with us.

Finally breaking free from the Akache commander's words in her mind, the Black woman returns to reality, taking in the mayhem that has since erupted around her. She struggles to keep Karnitu's bizarre monologue locked away in her soul – but the commander's power is too strong. The words find their way to the tip of the woman's tongue, forcing their way out. "It is time to fight." The overzealous woman lifts her fist high in the air, and as she does so, a blistering crackling takes over the sky, putting a pin in her aggression. The customers scatter like rats in all directions, dropping their groceries everywhere. Soda bottles explode, glass jars shatter, and soon enough, liquid coats the ground.

Outside, a small clustering group of Akache pods marry with the sky, crawling their way in and becoming one with the hostile atmosphere. The eyes of every single citizen out on the street turn toward the heavens, oddly mesmerized by the vibrant red mist that flows from each modtron ship. All of a sudden, the Akache's mothership makes itself visible, surrounded by hundreds of pods. The ship is astounding – shaped like an octagon and tinted gray in color, with monstrous glowing light panels embedded into the exterior. Etched into the belly of the overwhelming spacecraft is the letter "A" for

"Akache." The sight of the vessel nearly screams "impending doom" as it gets closer and closer, seeming to expand so much as to take over the entire dark, gloomy sky.

A throng of African Americans, joined by a few white Americans, rush toward the ship, doing their best to flag it down. Seemingly without a will of their own right now, the people cheer, drawing attention to themselves, some pleading to be whisked away on the mothership. The massive ship continues its trek until it hovers just above the waiting mob of citizens. Without warning, a large spotlight emits from the bottom of the ship, lighting up the sky and settling on the rowdy group.

Those in the spotlight wave their hands excitedly, signifying that an alien abduction would be a more pleasant experience than life in the United States. Everyone holds their breath for what seems like an eternity — until one by one, the feet of each willing citizen lift off the ground. Each person levitates in midair, somehow being pulled toward the ship through some unknown force. But something no one expects happens next… The melanin from the bodies of the Black Americans gets whisked away, entirely separating from their skin as they ascend toward the blaring spotlight. Joyous tears fill the eyes of these citizens. Others still on the ground spread their arms wide, ready to accept their fate with grace. The few white citizens ready to board the ship are suddenly frozen in midair and then abruptly cast down toward the ground.

"What the fuck! This is such bullshit," a white male objects as his body violently spirals back towards Earth. "This is bullshit. We are all one!" Every other white American floating toward the spaceship is gradually rejected, painfully tumbling back to the ground.

Standing on the side, taking it all in, is the Black woman from the grocery story. She watches from a secure spot, but a feeling of regret slowly creeps up on her. With a perplexed look on her face, she turns to the small group of white Americans. "Someone sees us. It's time we take back what's rightly owed to us." The woman steps out, allowing herself to be seen by the spotlight, and accepts her call to the unknown. Her body floats gracefully toward the mighty light.

Below stares a sea of white faces, each one of them rejected, as the mothership happily swallows up every last one of the willing African Americans. "What about us?"

Chapter 5
One by One

A large television screen stands tall in the middle of the White House's East Room. Nearly every last staff member of the White House gathers around, watching news reels that show African Americans levitating toward the beaming spotlights from the legion of Akache ships all over the country. Each staff member wears a look of disbelief. Bodies numb, heavy hearts racing, as the staff watches the footage with rapt attention.

Meanwhile, in the Oval Office, President Reid makes a private call. He slams the phone down for but a moment — and then picks it up again. He dials Science and Technology director, Mark Fitz. The President doesn't waste time on pleasantries. "Tell me about the research."

"It's going very well, Mr. President," Fitz replies from the other end of the line. "I have a small update. The kids' blood is extraordinary. Science hasn't seen anything like it. Our findings will help identify a frailty somewhere. Without having one of them in my lab, the closest we have is the teenager. I am not sure his affiliation is directly linked to them, but we can only hope."

"What do you mean?"

"We haven't tested their DNA, their molecular structure. We don't know how strong they are. Their makeup could offer resistance to our science… It's just an unknown, Mr. President."

"Mark, I took a risk, helping you secure that vial of blood. I fucking need answers, and quick." He puts the phone on speaker.

"Mr. President, I promise. Give me a few days."

President Reid stands up to pace the room, breathing deeply. Right outside the Oval Office, patrolling guards and Secret Service agents abound. The President stops pacing to look out one of the windows, but the agents immediately wave at him to get back. After a moment, he complies with their urgent request.

He steps back over to his desk chair. "Mark, we don't have 'days.' We are moments away from a catastrophe in our country."

"I understand that, Mr. President. You know as well as I that there will be collateral damage. It's the cornerstone of science — evolution."

President Reid silently takes in the unsolicited warning from Fitz. Again, he jumps to his feet, once more pacing the room. This time, he comes to a stop near a bust of

Abraham Lincoln. He stares intently at the bronzed masterpiece, wishing it would speak to him or in some way yield the answers he seeks. Fitz's voice shatters the President's concentration. Shaken out of his daydream, he returns to his desk, listening.

"Mr. President, you are privy to a host of intelligence… Could your team have known of this breach?"

"Mark, please. Provide an update soon."

"Sure thing, Mr. President." Before President Reid gets a chance to hang up, Fitz coyly sneaks in one last question. "One final thing. For decades, I've heard things about 'what's out there' beyond my work here as a scientist. Is there… Something more I should know?"

President Reid hesitates. His extended silence doesn't help his case, as far as Fitz is concerned. "No. Mark, you have all the information I have." He abruptly hangs up the phone. His fingertips on the Resolute desk, he gently taps against the cherry oak. Taking a moment to himself, the President settles down and contemplates the information that Fitz had just proposed. A knock on the door breaks his concentration. "Come in," President Reid calls out.

Right away the door swings open and in walks Molly, the President's Chief of Staff.

"Mr. President, you have to see this." The worried look on the woman's face and her defeated posture is enough to prompt the most powerful man in the world to hurl ass out of the Oval Office.

Back in the East Room, the staff members are still huddled together, clearly disturbed by what they have been watching. As the President rushes in, the staff disperses to either side of the quiet room, allowing him to get up close and personal with the television. With each step he takes, his eyes widen and his heart beats even more rapidly than the moment before. On the huge screen directly in front of him, he watches as African American bodies from all over the country float toward the deceptively welcoming light presented by each pod in the sky — to be suctioned up inside the ship just as their melanin gets torn away from their body.

The President looks horrified. "What in bloody hell is that?"

A feeling of dread has descended upon the room, and with each passing moment, the feeling grows heavier. A veteran hailing from Alabama, known for his neatly trimmed golden mane of hair and the awkward design of his freckles (a humorous conversation starter around the Pentagon), John Grossman, the President's Secretary of Defense, pipes up.

He looks toward the President with fear in his eyes and panic beating in his voice. "It has begun."

"How many Americans do they have?"

"Dallas, Flint, Louisiana, Newark… It's endless. We can't keep track of every ship. Our satellites can only see so much, Mr. President. They appear from out of nowhere."

"I want an estimate!"

An anxious hush falls over the crowd. They keep quiet, never having before witnessed the President raise his voice to anyone. Grossman hesitates. "Maybe a few million, Mr. President."

As he slowly grasps the gravity of the situation, defeat creeping into his mind, President Reid thrusts his tightly clenched fists against the arms of his chair. A grave look on his face sets in. He whispers something cold and daunting. "They are building an army."

"Who's to say… Maybe they'll take them back to where they came from," Grossman comments with a hint of sarcasm.

The President swiftly interjects, turning to face the contentious Secretary of Defense. "Take them back where, John?

Grossman looks back at his colleagues, from one side of the room to the other, hoping for someone to back up his brutally offensive commentary. But mum's the word for the rest of them. Grossman sidles up next to Molly, the Chief of Staff, whispering in her ear. "Come on, he knows we're all thinking it."

President Reid clears his throat to address the room with finality. "We don't know what or who they are. Some of our fellow Americans have opted to join them. We will not judge – until we have to." He walks out.

One mile underneath the White House, back at the secret room in which Caleb and Jaylen are still held captive, the two boys sit with their backs against the wall. The friends use their seemingly endless time stuck in this tiny room to discuss what might be left of their respective futures. Until now, they've watched a spider weave a web for who knows how many hours.

"You think she's dead?" Jaylen asks Caleb.

"Who?"

"Bree, dummy."

"I try not to think about it," Caleb replies, intent on changing the subject.

"No, seriously, Cal. You think they killed her?"

"I don't know, Jaylen. I try not to think about it."

A few moments pass. Jaylen pipes up again. "You liked her, huh?"

Caleb shifts his body on the ground, the cold concrete massaging his legs to sleep. "Yeah, she was cool."

Jaylen challenges the vague response. "Bro, you not going to answer the question?"

"Damn, Jaylen, why is it all or nothing with you? I told you how I felt."

"Calm down, Cal, it was just a question. Based on that reaction, no need to say any more."

"Whatever."

"You whatever," Caleb snaps back. The boys turn to one another and share a smile, the first smile they've shared in what feels like days. "They are strong, Jaylen."

"You ain't gotta tell me. I saw firsthand in that ship, Cal."

"But we're stronger."

Jaylen spins around to face his friend again, a puzzled smirk curling his lips. "Why do you always defend these hateful cowards in America?"

"I'm not defending people like that... I'm speaking up for people like you and me."

"Look... Peaceful protests got MLK a bullet in his head. Why would we be any different? If we want a different outcome, we got to do things different." Caleb tilts his head just enough to block the annoying light emanating from the overhead bulb. Jaylen continues. "When I was on the ship, the commander said something that made a lot of sense. I didn't want to believe him. The core of my being said he was right, but my heart said he was wrong."

"What did he say?"

"The Akache philosophy is that of potent lineage and scarce resources. The adversity that abounds within our culture cultivates this 'B' gene in us, deeming us an anomaly of some kind. They know how to hone in on its power." Jaylen hops to his feet, excitement suddenly hurling him around the room with glee. "Bro, I saw how you glided us down from that ship, and what you did in front of the White House. You definitely got that gene."

"No, Jaylen, we all do."

"You think we can take a bank with it? Like Cleo in Set It Off... Get all the money—"

Caleb reaches up and yanks Jaylen back to the ground with him, stalling his enthusiasm. "It's bigger than money, Jay. Don't you get it? They are going to use us for their bidding."

Jaylen shrugs his shoulders, clearly not understanding the importance of Caleb's words. "So?"

"So, first, it's White America. Once they get what they want, we would be on the chopping block next."

"You are definitely pulling at fucking straws, Cal."

"I give up," Caleb says, defeated.

Jaylen's excitement revs up again. He vigorously pounds his fist into his palm. "Good. We young men – let's join the fight. Who needs followers when you got Akache! Did I pronounce their name correctly?"

Suddenly the white spots on Caleb's arm ever so slowly begin to regenerate. Jaylen's the first to notice. "Cal, your arm…" Caleb looks down and releases a mighty screech. The next moment, his body begins shaking uncontrollably. "Caleb, bro, don't do this again. Help!!"

"I've got to get out of here. It wants me dead!"

"What? Who?"

From outside the metal enclosure of the secret room, excruciating screams echo throughout the deserted corridor.

Chapter 6
It's a Secret Service

The door to the secret room gently creaks open. Caleb's unconscious body spills out and half-collapses into the arms of a Secret Service agent. In the doorway, Jaylen appears behind Caleb, doing his best to hold up his friend, and failing miserably.

"You gotta help him. He won't last down here much longer. He needs to see a doctor," Jaylen pleads to the agent with a look of desperation on his face as he cradles his friend.

Caleb's skin has dulled into a sort of grayish hue, his body lacks the strength to hold himself upright, and his breathing is labored and sporadic. His eyes are open, unblinking, giving off an eerie look of imminent death.

The agent takes his sweet time looking the two teens up and down, his expression radiating an intimidating gaze. He lazily radios for backup.

Soon after, Caleb and Jaylen join the agent at the elevator just outside the secret room as it heads upward toward the White House. Caleb's arm is draped over Jaylen's shoulder as Jaylen does the best he can to carry the extra weight.

The elevator doors slide open to reveal a crowded hall filled with military personnel. All of a sudden, every single pair of eyes in that hallway locks onto Caleb and Jaylen. Everyone desperately wants to catch a glimpse of the two boys who managed to breach the most secure building in the world. Several agents stand by, waiting impatiently to scold the teens — but they reconsider their next steps once taking into consideration Caleb's shocking state of health. One of the White House aides hands a shirt to Jaylen, which he uses to cover up Caleb's exposed chest.

Under the watchful eyes of the trigger-happy agents, the boys stagger up the packed hallway. Soon, Caleb's breathing steadies. He gradually musters up enough energy to gather himself a bit.

"Well, don't just stand there — help us," Jaylen demands to the agents surrounding them. No luck. The four stocky agents keep their distance, refusing to assist, and instead point in the direction of the in-house medical office. His strength starting to wane, Jaylen alone continues, struggling to get Caleb to safety as quick as possible. But suddenly, the weight of Caleb's body becomes too much for him, and both teens take a spill right in the middle of the hallway.

After a few moments on the floor, Caleb's strength and smooth chocolate skin tone are somehow restored. All ailments he was battling with vanish into thin air. "I think I'm okay, Jaylen. I don't know what that was, but it's gone. It wouldn't let go."

Jaylen helps Caleb to his feet. Remembering that they're being watched like animals in cages, the boys turn around to find smug looks from the surrounding agents.

"What's crawled up their butt?" Jaylen quips.

"Please, Jaylen, let's keep our cool. Maybe we can get out of this."

The boys make their way to the East Room. They find the White House staff, still glued to the television as it shows invasion news coverage. Jaylen elbows his way through the group for a closer look at the television. He stands right in front.

"Whoa, Cal, look at that." Jaylen watches, mesmerized. Staff members move their heads to see around Jaylen, not daring to take their eyes off the screen even for a second. Horrifying images fill the television as Akache ships cast foreboding shadows, flooding the nighttime skies. White

Americans do their best to flee the invasions, taking cover in their homes for fear of the unknown.

Caleb's eyes widen in terror, for he's seen things. He knows what kind of future lies ahead unless the Akache invaders are stopped.

"This is only the beginning," he whispers, just barely loud enough for himself to hear. Yet, somehow Secretary of Defense Grossman managed to read his lips…

"What did you say, son?"

"I didn't say anything," Caleb reassures him.

"You sure, boy?"

Jaylen steps in front of his friend. His natural instincts will forever lead him to protect Caleb, even though he's younger by only a few months. "Who are you calling 'boy'?"

One by the one the head of each staff member turns toward Jaylen, the sudden commotion overpowering the shock from the on-screen devastation. Fear has never been an issue for Jaylen throughout his life thus far — he's grown to accept that his mouth just always seems to get him into trouble. "You would think we would get more respect now that Akache is about to be in that ass…"

Caleb tugs on Jaylen's shirt, pleading with him. "Jaylen, no."

"Naw, Cal, these fools got to know what the deal is."

Grossman steps in to entertain Jaylen's proposal. "And who are you?"

"I'm Jaylen, and that's Caleb. My homie got gifts. Y'all don't wanna mess with him."

Caleb grabs a fistful of Jaylen's shirt collar and nudges him off to the side, away from the group. The following murmurs that leave his mouth are soft but unforgiving. "Jay, you are making a fool out of us. Shut up!"

Grossman overhears the boys' little side chat. "No, go on, let him talk. Tell us, Jaylen. What else do you know?" The man's booming words drip with sarcasm.

A sobering silence falls over the room as every eye gazes at Jaylen, the skinny kid from Lanier University with the mighty tongue. Several of the staff members hold up their smartphones, stealthily filming. Jaylen has secured center stage for right now, and he's loving it.

He puffs out his chest, the raspiness in his voice cutting through the silence, making his commentary even more daunting to his audience. "The world is about to change as we know it, and there is nothing America can do about it. I look at that screen, watching those folks running for cover, not knowing what the future will bring. Try living that way every day." A fragment of inner turmoil snakes its way into Jaylen's speech. He fights back tears and manages to console himself enough to finish the grand declaration. "You are going to find out real soon what it means to be without freedom."

The exchange between Jaylen and Grossman is reminiscent of watching a tennis match. Staff members stare, respectfully taking in the perspectives of both sides.

"And how sure are you about that?" Grossman asks.

"Things have been changing for some time now. Look around the room. We are not here because you think we don't belong here." Jaylen's truth guts the staff members to their core. Some even hang their head in shame. "My father always said to give man, humanity, a chance to prove his or her integrity. We've waited a long time, and we can't wait anymore." Pleased with himself, the sly grin on his face signifying utter bliss, Jaylen turns back to the television, watching as the metallic ships dance across the pitch black sky.

Now Caleb's the one in the hot seat. Grossman and the others focus on him, patiently waiting for his statement. Caleb steps into the center of the room, eyeing each staff member as they stare right back. He awkwardly glances up at the crystal chandelier dangling overhead, taking in the monumental moment of this peculiar, yet groundbreaking, occasion. Thinking back, Caleb would have sworn that this eventual White House visit would be a joyous, welcoming one — but that is not the case, so instead, he accepts the circumstances and begins.

"I am Caleb Prescott. I was a freshman at HBCU Lanier University." Caleb nods toward the television screen. "Several years ago 'they' visited me. I don't know how or why." His eyes slowly flutter shut. "I can feel them. They are strong, like nothing I've ever felt before."

Grossman suddenly grows wary from Caleb's longwinded explanation. He loosens his necktie as casually as he can. "Why haven't they attacked us?"

Caleb's eyes peel open. The staff members wait patiently for his reply, but even they could never prepare for the words that would follow. "Because I haven't allowed them to."

Some look on with confused smirks, unsure what to think. Grossman shoots a sideways glance to the the bulky Secret

Service agents still lurking in the doorway. "What are you saying? Are you their liaison?"

"No. I don't think so."

"What do they want?"

"They want the thing that you have and are unwilling to give up… Power."

"Will they hurt us?"

"I wish I can tell you 'no.'"

All at once the entire White House staff congregates behind Grossman, as though mentally urging him to ask deeper, more probing questions. They need all the information they can get.

"How do we stop them?" Grossman prods.

"You can't."

The room erupts in chaos at those two terrifying words. Grossman hushes the staff, and the chatter settles down. "You expect the United States Government to believe that what you're saying is fact?"

"What you decide to do with the information I've given you is on you."

With that, Jaylen's had enough. He wedges his foot in between Caleb and the Secretary of Defense. "I bet if he were some white teen, you'd think he was telling the truth, right? Y'all brought this war to our doorstep. Now we've decided to open the door."

Caleb looks toward the window and wanders over. Peering out at the fleet of ships hiding under the cover of night, his mind drifts along into a faraway realm. “There is a gene called ‘Belivian’ in every Black American. The majority doesn’t know they have it. It’s something we are born with and can’t be taken away. For a while, it’s been dormant.” Caleb steps back from the window and points to the pods hovering overhead. “They have found a way to revive and nurture that gene. It took them hundreds of years to find us. They’ve searched for human atrocities around the universe until they found our little planet.”

“Why should we believe you?”

“Even if you wanted to believe what I’ve shared, you wouldn’t,” Caleb retorts, swinging around to face Grossman, a sadness in his eyes now apparent. “Sir, you ever wonder why it takes so much intense pressure to make a diamond? The funny part is that it takes the same amount of pressure to make dust. I bet you are wondering what all that means. At times, I get lost in it myself. Akache has one shot — they know it, and they will take that shot. That’s what I'm afraid of.” Caleb steals another glance at the television, nervously watching as African Americans float toward the ships while manic chaos ensues throughout the rest of the continent.

"What could they possibly want with those people?" Grossman asks, an evil smirk on his face. "Most of them are poor, uneducated, and hopeless."

"Hope breeds faith, sir. It is better to be of a lowly spirit with the poor than to divide the spoils with the proud. Akache will turn their pain into fury… Their despair into triumph…"

"Whose side are you on?"

"There are no such things as 'sides,' only choices. When the time comes, we will all have to make a choice."

Those final words trigger something deep within Grossman. He instantly loses all of his cool, snatching up Caleb by the shirt and berating him with the foulest obscenities. "You are a fucking liar!" The angry man's fist inches closer and closer to Caleb's face as the rest of the room watches in horror.

Chapter 7
What Are You Hiding?

Caleb uses his forearm to shield his face from Secretary of Defense Grossman's closed fist as it propels forward, closer and closer.

At exactly the right moment, President Reid's hand shoots out, halting the force of Grossman's fierce blow. "What in God's name are you doing?"

"I'm protecting our country, Mr. President," Grossman explains. "This punk kid and his friend are in on this invasion. It's my right as an American to put an end to terrorism."

The President surveys the room, daring anyone else to step forward in agreement with Grossman's uncouth vigilante approach. When everyone avoids making eye contact, the President turns back to Grossman. "I demand your resignation on my desk immediately, Secretary Grossman."

"You can't do that," the conceited Grossman says.

"I just did." President Reid gives an affirming nod to the Secret Service agents standing inside the doorway. The burly agents threateningly surround the highest official in the military as though he were a stranger off the street.

"Are you out of your mind? These galactic terrorists will tear this country apart," Grossman babbles.

After once again having held his tongue for as long as he can stand, Jaylen finds the perfect opening. "We aren't the ones you should be worried about."

Grossman scoffs. "I've done more for this country than you'll ever know." On the inside, he fumes with desire to continue his assault on the teens.

Feeling himself and ready to stand up for what's right, Jaylen shakes an accusing finger at the unapologetic man. "Yeah, that's the running theme with you former politicians… Start a war, never fight in the war, boast about your weak policies, and then start another war to mask your failures." Jaylen huffs with disgust.

"I am a five-star general— Wait, why am I explaining my credentials to some thug?" Grossman takes a moment and manages to get it together. Wanting to leave the premises with what little is left of his integrity, he adjusts his tie and pushes his glasses deeper into the bridge of his nose. He spews his last words. "Mr. President, you'll be sorry." The agents roughly escort Grossman out of the East Room.

President Reid spins on his heels to address the remaining staff members. The chaos settles down and a thick, heavy silence falls over the room. "I am asking for your commitment in the fight against this unknown faction. If this is a problem, please, you are free to leave."

Each staff member weighs their options, debating whether or not to stay. Some whisper to one another. After some deliberating, two senior Cabinet members march out the door in rebellion, departing without a single word, neither of explanation nor farewell.

"Anyone else? You are free to go."

Those who remain signify their stance in solidarity with the President's mission. The President nods and regains his usual sense of reserve, forcing the upsetting frown off his face. He silently leaves the East Room.

Sprinting after him a moment later is Caleb and Jaylen – but a handful of watchful agents swiftly snatch up the two boys by the collar, stopping them from keeping up. "President Reid, wait!" Caleb shouts.

President Reid pauses and turns, taking in the scene. He gives his agents the signal, placing his palm out in front of him. The beefy agents release the boys.

As soon as their feet touch the ground, Caleb and Jaylen race up the lengthy hall, trying to catch their breath in the process. "Wait," Caleb implores. "I can help."

The President stares back at the teens, irritated, his arms set across his chest. "What is it?"

Caleb reaches within a few feet of President Reid and comes to a stop. He carefully observes the President's disagreeable body language, the astute teen taking mental notes before releasing his next sentence. "Your Secretary of Defense asked me a very poignant question that I'd like to ask you."

"Go on," President Reid says. "I'll entertain your inquiry."

"Why haven't you attacked the ships?"

Jaylen fumes with rage. "True that! America attacks everything else – why not them?!"

Caleb keeps a close eye on the President, who stumbles over his carefully chosen statement of contrivance. "I know what you're getting at, son, but this moment is like no other."

"What about the one million Black Americans... Did they matter?"

President Reid takes a stand; the same stand he took during every Cabinet meeting concerning the optics of the Melanin Experiment. "I fight for every American, no matter the creed, race, or political affiliation." With that, he's had enough of the questions. He turns and walks off in the opposite direction.

Caleb's eyes settle on the gold embroidery of the bright red carpet beneath his feet, distracting himself as he lands his next verbal blow. "I believe you are not telling us everything. It's just a hunch I have," Caleb touts with a more serious inflection in his voice. He continues studying the President's nonverbal cues, hoping that a hint of any kind would jump out at him.

President Reid freezes for a moment, then turns back to face Caleb. The most powerful man in the Free World has been involved in many heated exchanges with foreign adversaries all around the world – but nothing has quite prepared him for such incessant questioning from one particular teen boy.

Jaylen nudges closer to Caleb. He sneaks a whisper into his ear. "Dude, he's hiding something. Don't trust him."

After some hesitation, the President's eyes sweep from the boys to his swarm of strategically positioned Secret Service agents not far off in the distance. "I've said what I'm allowed to say."

A startling rumble thunders beneath the feet of everyone in the hallway. It momentarily shifts the weight of President Reid and the boys, providing a welcome reprieve to their uncomfortable exchange.

Jaylen looks toward Caleb, arching one of his brows. "What was that?"

All of a sudden, a sharp pain radiates from deep within Caleb's chest. The stabbing sensation sends him back a few paces as he clutches one side of his chest in agony. "Damn it."

President Reid observes as Caleb's pain seemingly jumps from one side of his chest to the other, with no determinable pattern. "Are you okay, fellow?"

"I don't know. I've got to get home. I feel safer there." Caleb struggles to choke out the words.

The President shakes his head dismissively. "I can't do that. You are our eyes into their world. You two stay put."

Not having it, Jaylen steps in front of Caleb, focusing on the view of the pale President, deep worry lines embedded into his perfectly wrinkled face. "I'm with Caleb. You aren't telling us everything. We are no more than pawns in your games of war and systemic racist legislation. I've followed you, Adam. Your past isn't squeaky clean!"

President Reid remains silent, feigning any willingness or desire to hear this out.

Jaylen carries on. "As a senator in the South, you attached yourself to a racist bill that forced schools to take up the legislation. It's funny what stays on the internet forever…"

"Not true," President Reid rebuts. "I voted against it. Look, your country needs you more than ever, son."

"Very TRUE, Adam Reid. Did my country need me when the cops shot my father in the center of the street in cold blood?" The hallways goes silent as passersby sneak wistful glances in Jaylen's direction. "It was a lottery ticket! A lottery ticket! They 'thought' it was a gun!" Flowing tears carve a path down Jaylen's chocolate skin. His words morph respectfully into shouts of pain, coming from deep within his core. He has waited years to address the sickening truth he's endured, realizing in this very moment that escaping it was never a possibility. "Fuck America and all its racist history. I hate this country." Jaylen forces out his last statement through the lump in his throat. "Why can't it ever just be fair?"

Not knowing what else to do, Caleb reaches out and embraces his friend. Jaylen at first resists, pulling away slightly before giving into the extended hug. This moment represents the very liberation of Jaylen's soul, the true realization of acceptance that he is never going to see his father again. President Reid keeps his physical distance but his soul remains quiet, moved beyond belief at the teen's declaration.

Words of clarity find a home on Caleb's tongue. "We have to go. Let us go. Please," he pleads again.

Keeping silent, President Reid absorbs the torturous pain communicated through the sound of Jaylen's despairing cry. The powerful man inhales a whiff of the anguish that lingers like a thick fog, suffocating everything in its path. He contemplates Caleb's plea, abandoning his authority. Finally… "You are free to leave." President Reid gives a last nod to his agents before walking away.

The eerie nighttime sky fades with the break of a bright new day as an official government SUV with tinted windows speeds down the road. Two more government vehicles trail behind, each maintaining a sizable distance. In the backseat of the SUV leading the way sit Caleb and Jaylen, nerves ablaze as they wait to be returned home. The friends haven't said as much as two words within the last hour since being released as captives from the White House.

"Jaylen, you okay?" Caleb whispers.

Jaylen looks out the window, mindlessly staring into the sun's blinding rays. Anything to help him stop thinking about the pain fighting him on the inside. "I'm cool, bro."

Caleb turns to Jaylen with a sharp look. "I know when you're lying. You are not 'cool.'"

"Well, what shall I say, Cal?"

"Say you'll be okay."

"You don't know what they took from me, Cal. You still got your father." Jaylen sits in his sorrow, using the feeling as an excuse to drift away into a memory of happier times. "He was showing me how to parallel park that morning, 'cause I was horrible at it… Po-po pulls up, looking for trouble. My dad had a temper. He gets out of the car." The teen pauses, trying to suck the sadness back in. He pokes out his chest and fights through it. "They shot him. They shot him."

"I'm sorry, bro." Caleb hangs his head.

"Don't be. They weren't."

Sorrow hangs heavy in the air for a long moment. Caleb jabs himself in the chest. "It's gone… The pain."

"I wish I could say the same, Cal."

"You can. Sometimes you have to let it come through you before it will go away."

"Okay, 'Doctor Fucking Phil.'"

Caleb gets a serious look on his face. Jaylen sees him out of the corner of his eyes. "No, I'm just a friend who wants his homie to be okay."

"Don't do that mushy stuff right now… Can I bask in my hatred for another fifteen minutes, please?

"No. I believe we can stop them."

"Are you insane?! How? Besides, it's probably better we unite with Akache like the others."

The SUV unexpectedly swerves to the left, then to the right. The teens in the backseat bang from one end and back to the other. As the car skids to a screeching halt, their young bodies slam against the back of the driver and passenger seat. Lying in a twisted mess on the car's floor, Caleb and Jaylen struggle to get upright. The agent driving is unconscious.

"That's some terrible driving," Jaylen remarks.

Opening one of the car doors, the boys escape outside, plagued by new aches and pains. Slowly, they look up and discover a fleet of Akache pods now blocking their path.

Chapter 8
Home Sweet Home

It's the crack of dawn. A fleet of Akache pods dance overhead, taunting anyone unlucky enough to be caught up in their overwhelming presence. They begin their descent, landing on the road with the intent to block traffic from either direction. Caleb and Jaylen watch — half in awe, half in terror — as the metallic ships settle just several yards away from them. They're trapped. Secret Service agents rapidly pile out of their cars, their guns drawn, aiming right for the immobile spacecraft squadron.

"Don't shoot, please," Caleb pleads with the agents. He begins to approach the fleet. Jaylen stays behind, waiting to see how the moment plays out.

"Cal, what are you doing, bro?"

"I'm going to reason with them… Someone has to." Caleb cautiously takes several more measured steps forward, getting closer. Everyone watches curiously as a faint red mist seeps out from the top of each ship and disappears into the atmosphere.

"What is that?" Jaylen wonders.

"Stay quiet, Jay," Caleb says in a hushed tone.

The agents keep tabs on Caleb from afar, using their vehicles as barriers between themselves and the foreign ships. Now just a mere step away from the fleet, Caleb's brown inquisitive eyes examine the massive metallic hardware that stands before him. His mind races as he takes mental notes regarding the ships' beautiful craftsmanship. He takes in the colorful effervescence of the light pockets cemented to each ship's surface. Slowly, he ventures closer still. The red mist, he notices, gives off a delightfully sweet scent that's similar to honey. It seductively dances below his nostrils, drawing him in.

The anxious teen rests a palm on one of the ships' surface. Without warning, the electrifying sensation of a sparking current sends a subtle wave of warmth through Caleb's mocha skin. Absorbing the powerful surge somehow comes natural to him, and he accepts it, taking it all in without a struggle. It takes not even a moment to activate something deep within Caleb's essence. First, his left eye fades from its mysterious deep brown to a washed-out gray tone. Next, his shoulders spring to attention, followed by a height boost of a few inches, unnoticeable to those off in the distance.

By now, Jaylen's sought protection from the agents, using them to shield himself from the unknown. "Caleb, what are you doing?"

Caleb doesn't respond to Jaylen. Instead, he is transfixed, seemingly paralyzed. But then his mouth opens. The voice that emerges is one of a foreign language – rich, bold, and precise as it chants. "Aca mei consto adelia." The agents watch, still from afar, holding their fire, waiting for someone or something to materialize.

Jaylen tries again. "Caleb? Caleb??"

Dark tatted markings begin forming on Caleb's body, tracing down his arms and then appearing across his neck. Internally, he feels stronger, taller, and fully in control. "Aca mei consto adelia," he chants again.

This time, Caleb's chant prompts the fleet of ships to return to the sky, once again allowing traffic to pass. Everyone watches in shock.

A blond agent with a severe crew cut and an unsavory attitude marches over to Caleb. "You communicated with them. What did they say? Tell us now!"

Caleb comes out of it, shaking himself free from his self-induced trance. The bold markings on his face and body dissipate slightly. "I won't be able to control them much longer."

"What do you mean?" snaps the snide agent.

"They are gearing up for a battle of a lifetime. One that will cost lives." The agent says nothing, fighting the urge to refute the foreboding revelations Caleb has just spoken. "There is only one way to save us."

Jaylen steps out from behind one of the hulking agents to lock eyes with his friend. "How?"

"Become one of them."

One hour later, the motorcade arrives at its destination, pulling up in front of Caleb's childhood home. His house sits tucked away at the end of a cul-de-sac in an affluent part of town, miles north of Washington. The neighborhood as a whole is pretty tame, with the highest form of entertainment being its annual Girl Scout cookies extravaganza.

Caleb and Jaylen exit the SUV, looking back to watch the disgruntled agents watching them as they make their way up to the house's entrance. Jaylen gives a playful wave. "See ya, fellas!"

Snarling, the agent with the crew cut shouts from the vehicle. "We got orders. You two stay put!" The procession of SUVs eerily line the cul-de-sac. It's clear they aren't going anywhere. The main agent sits back in his cushioned seat, lights a cigarette, and waits.

Seemingly home free, the boys sprint for the house, leaping up onto the porch just like they did as kids; a friendly competition they've shared since childhood.

Jaylen's eyes widen as he notices the advancement in Caleb's leap — several inches higher than ever before. "Damn, bro, your ups are legit these days! Cheating ass!"

Caleb smirks coyly at Jaylen as he bangs on the front door. "Dad! Dad!" Someone carefully pulls open the door.

All of a sudden, Mr. Prescott, Caleb's dad, charges out of the house, hugging him as though it had been years. "I was so worried, son. God, I prayed for your safety…" The delighted father looks his son up and down with an adoring gaze. As his paternal instinct kicks in, he realizes there is something different about his son — but his elation stalls his curiosity. Mr. Prescott turns to Jaylen, grabbing him up in a hug with the same level of elation. "Jaylen. I prayed for your safety too, buddy."

"You did?"

"Yes, sure I did. You're my son as well."

Jaylen doesn't fare well when it comes to dealing with his emotions, so he offers Mr. Prescott an awkward fist bump instead.

"Where's Bree?" Mr. Prescott asks, searching the walkway as if expecting that she might be lagging behind. "Her parents are worried sick about her."

The boys exchange a glance with one another, both unsure of how to explain the lack of Bree's presence. Caleb abruptly pivots, changing the subject. "Dad, we are really tired."

"And hungry," Jaylen adds.

Mr. Prescott eyes the caravan of cars clogging up the entire cul-de-sac. "Who are they?"

"It's a long story, Dad…"

Mr. Prescott ushers in the boys, securing the front door behind them. As soon as they set foot inside, Jaylen makes a beeline for the kitchen. He nearly disappears inside the refrigerator, quickly emerging with several plates piled with food in his hands. Meanwhile, Caleb sits at the dining table, comforted by the familiar aroma of vanilla-scented candles ablaze throughout the house. When Caleb's mother died, Mr. Prescott helped his son cope through their new nightly process of lighting candles around the house to honor his mother and remember her life. Outdated newspapers and magazines clutter up the sofa in the living room across the way. Mounted on almost every wall in the three-bedroom house are article clippings. Piles of grocery bags have been stuffed in corners all throughout the house. A massive calendar sits plastered to the wall, featuring big, bold lettering signifying particular dates and events. From his seat at the table, Caleb examines every inch of his childhood home, somewhat shocked by its current state. His eyes follow along the trails of papers resting at his feet, just one of many paper stacks in the immediate vicinity. Caleb recalls his father's peculiar approach to deciphering information – but this is a bit much, even for him. Mr. Prescott walks over to one of the windows, carefully peeking out the blinds for a glimpse at the waiting Secret Service agents. With a concerned look on his face, he takes a seat at the table, settling right across from Caleb.

"Caleb, what did you do?"

"It's more like what didn't he do," Jared yells from the refrigerator with a mouth full of food. The ravenous teen joins Caleb and Mr. Prescott a few moments later, crowding the table with various kinds of fruit, plates of meats, and a number of sugary snacks.

"Caleb, there are six vehicles out there with White House plates," Mr. Prescott eyes the boys intensely. "What did you two do?"

"I wish I could say 'nothing,' Dad," Caleb says, hanging his head. "But I can't."

Mr. Prescott nods, gingerly lifting himself from the table. He heads for a towering tan cabinet just off the living room. A modest assortment of guns is nestled inside the cabinet. First, he grabs a 9mm handgun and stuffs it into his pants. Next, he pulls down a shotgun and hangs it from his shoulder. Mr. Prescott returns to the boys at the table, nonchalantly reclaiming his seat. "Start from the beginning," he says.

Caleb rolls up a slice of deli turkey and stuffs it into his mouth. He's familiar with this quirky side of his father, so he's unbothered. "It's hard to explain, Dad."

"Son, are you in trouble?"

"No."

"Does this have something to do with what happened at the HBCUs?"

"Sort of.

Jaylen digs into a box of donut holes, chomping away at the delicious treats, popping them into his mouth one by one. "I'll explain it, Mr. Prescott." Jaylen rattles off the recent turn of events like it's nothing. "The Melanin Experiment wasn't a hoax. They, as in the Akache invaders, are siding with us Black people. The President is hiding something. Caleb may have superpowers—

oh, and do you have any more of those lemon drops you always buy?"

Mr. Prescott looks confused. He rises from the table, curiously scratching at his scalp while going over Jaylen's rapid explanation in his head. "Caleb, what is he talking about?"

"Dad, I'm really tired. I need to rest."

For the first time, Mr. Prescott commands the room. The pitch of his voice intensifies, releasing a punishing tone that brings him back to the days of living under his own father's roof as a rebellious teen. "No, not until you explain what's going on. Is the government in on this?"

"Yup," Jaylen confidently affirms, still feasting.

"I knew this day would come, but I didn't think it would come this soon…" Mr. Prescott fills his shotgun with bullets in preparation.

Caleb eyes the gun worriedly. "Dad, what are you doing?"

"I've always warned you about this, Caleb. You always have to be ready. The government is not your friend. They will take you OUT!" Caleb stares as his father spins out into a hyped rant about the disturbing state of the government. "Son, when I sent you to school, I knew it was a matter of time before something happened. Those digitally animated ships they're showing on television aren't real."

"Dad, they are real," Caleb disputes.

"Stop it, Caleb. You're only sixteen… You don't know what I know."

"But Dad—"

"No. I have a duty to protect my own at all costs."

Caleb's heard more than he can stand. He slams both of his fists onto the table, getting everyone's attention. "Dad, will you listen, please? You don't know what you're talking about."

Jaylen backs up Caleb, chomping on an apple. "Mr. Prescott, Cal is right. They're real."

"Okay, okay," Mr. Prescott starts. "I'll entertain this. You are a college student with an opinion. Tell me more."

"Okay, well, they're called—"

"Wait." Mr. Prescott darts toward the television, grabbing the remote to power it on. He sets the volume as high as it can go. The paranoid man turns on an old radio. Earth, Wind & Fire's "September" blasts through the speakers. Turning back to the boys, Mr. Prescott mouths a few unintelligible words while pointing to the back door of the house. Jaylen snatches up a package of cookies off the table before following Mr. Prescott and Caleb through the door onto the patio. Several yards away at the back of the house is a brown shed, the kind you'd see on a farm. Caleb and Jaylen follow Mr. Prescott into the shed.

The cramped space of the shed is packed with even more newspapers. A few garden tools hang on the wall.

"It's really tight in here," Jaylen complains.

Mr. Prescott brings his index finger up to meet his lips, silently scolding the expressive teen. "Shhhhh…" A large rug sits in the center of the shed's floor. Mr. Prescott lifts it to reveal a metal hatch seamlessly obscured underneath.

Jaylen can't contain himself. "Whoa, what's that?!"

"Shhhhhhh," Mr. Prescott says as he opens the portable hatch, which drops off into pitch darkness. He leads the way into the black hole, utilizing a sleek metal ladder to lower himself down. Slowly but surely, all three reach the bottom of the unfamiliar pit. The first down, Mr. Prescott grabs a lantern and lights it with a match. A wall of canned goods, cots, blankets, and other survival essentials surrounds the dimly lit space.

Caleb's jaw drops at the sight. "Whoa, Dad, I never knew this was here."

"You weren't supposed to," Mr. Prescott says, casting a sidelong glance at his son. "Boys, you could live here for a year and be okay."

Jaylen walks along the space, eyes wide, taking it all in like a kid in a candy store. He stops at a mysteriously tiny door set in the East corner of the hideaway. "What's in here?"

Mr. Prescott follows Jaylen's gaze. "Never mind that." He turns to face Caleb. "Caleb, it's safe to talk down here."

Caleb begins his chilling info dump regarding the skyward invaders. The three gather in a circle as if sharing stories around a campfire. "Okay. They're called 'Akache,' an alien life-form from beyond the universe. They want to eradicate the white race in America."

"What?" Mr. Prescott inquires skeptically.

"Yes, they have specific orders, administered by their leader, Karnitu. The war is inevitable."

"Wait, let me get this straight… The ships are real. These aliens came to America and want to do away with white people. If true, I'm sure they'll make a movie about this shit."

"Yes," Caleb continues, "but I sense that there is something else pulling me, trying to control me."

Jaylen grabs a container of canned peaches from one of the shelves, opens the pull-tab, and inhales the contents. "You see, Mr. Prescott, I don't see the problem with their plot. If this is true, why not just let the shit happen?"

While Mr. Prescott struggles to make sense of what he's just been told, Caleb removes his shirt, exposing the markings on his back. His dad remains silent, eyes examining the intricate writings. "I've never seen anything like it. Who else knows about this?"

"The government knows, but they are in denial, like with most things," Jaylen says with a frown. "They don't understand how strong they are."

Mr. Prescott's head whips around to Jaylen. "Wait! You've seen them?"

"Yes, we both have, and to be truly honest, they look badass." Jaylen poses and flexes like a superhero.

"I think I can reason with them," Caleb assures.

"Caleb, you're a sixteen-year-old boy. Leave this to America to figure out."

"Dad, I tried, but they'll screw it up."

Jaylen wags an agreeable finger at Mr. Prescott. "If Caleb's assessment is correct and they only want to harm white Americans, why should we get involved?"

Mr. Prescott eyes Jaylen, digging deep inside himself to find the most honest words suitable for the occasion. "Because they'll come for us next. Nothing in life is free, boys… You'll always have a cross to bear."

A startling male voice penetrates through the darkness. "Hello?!!! Who's down there?"

"Quiet, boys. They've found us."

"Dad, we got to get out of here," Caleb whispers hoarsely.

Mr. Prescott springs into action. He points to the miniature door in the corner. "Crawl through there. It will take you past the Harrisons' house and underneath the farmer's market at the end of town."

Jaylen stares in shock. "You did a lot of digging, Mr. Prescott."

"Hurry, go!"

"Dad, come with us."

Mr. Prescott stares down at his son, his eyes scrubbing over every feature, each nuance, filing it away into his memory for good. He tries to shake the thought of never seeing his son again – but it doesn't budge.

Caleb presses. "I won't let them take you."

"I'll be fine, Caleb. You two take care of each other."

"But Dad!"

"No! Go!"

Jaylen grabs Caleb by the arm and forces him inside the small hole with him. Caleb looks over his shoulder, sneaking one last glimpse of his father, and mouths, "I love you." Mr. Prescott acknowledges his son's gesture with a subtle wave and a nod before removing his 9mm from his pants waistband. He isn't ready to concede without a fight. Caleb and Jaylen haul ass, crawling through the dark escape route toward safety.

From behind, the terrifying sound of gunshots cuts through the silence, paralyzing the boys in place.

Chapter 9
To Begin Again

Sounds of heavy breathing and panting echo from one end of the gloomy tunnel to the other. For the two boys, the hidden passageway is an eerie reminder of their escape through Lanier University's underground tunnel just days before. As his mind races with ideas of what might have happened to his father, Caleb's speed crawl putters to a stop.

"Caleb, keep going." Jaylen prods him from up ahead. "I can smell those bastards right behind us." A glaring spotlight cascades down the length of the tunnel, landing just inches from Caleb's feet. Panic sets in on Caleb's face as he fears the worst of what might come next.

"Bro, they are hot on our tails — keep going," Jaylen says, picking up the pace. Spooked, Caleb follows, urgently retreating deeper into the confined space. Each breath comes harder, faster as he struggles to find the remaining pockets of oxygen concealed within the darkness.

"Come on, Caleb. We're almost there."

Soon enough, the boys reach a door, one that's just big enough for a child to maneuver through. A sturdy classic wheel lock is secured to the door's surface. Jaylen tries his hand at turning the wheel, but the mechanism won't budge.

Caleb turns back, temporarily frozen in fear by the threat of the encroaching spotlight. Distant voices creep closer and closer from behind with each passing second.

"Come on, Caleb. Give a brother a hand," Jaylen says. The approaching voices goad Caleb into moving forward, and he springs into action, moving to help Jaylen. Summoning every ounce of strength, the boys furiously clench their teeth and grip the metal wheel attached to the door. They apply pressure to the locking mechanism, exerting themselves with such force that their faces quickly change from their natural brown to a vivid shade of red. The wheel begins to turn, slowly twisting open. Loud, offensive creaks from each turn of the stubborn mechanism ripple down the tunnel.

"It's moving. It's moving. Keep turning, Caleb," Jaylen says, breathlessly. Again, they hear faint voices behind them, closing in faster and faster.

Caleb freaks out. "Come on, Jaylen, turn!" Finally, a loud clank rings out as the wheel unlocks. Every step of the way, Caleb looks over his shoulder, expecting to see their assailants. The boys reposition, sitting on their bums to gain leverage — they kick open the metal door. Contorting their bodies as best they can, Caleb and Jaylen crawl through the small opening. What's obscured is a claustrophobic room suited to comfortably fit one adult. The teens squeeze their way inside. Caleb immediately reaches for the metal latch and locks the door behind them, making their getaway complete. Suffocating, at best, the tiny room is just high enough for the boys to stand up but not wide enough for them to stand together without their noses touching.

"Bro, why you so close?" Jaylen asks, annoyed.

"Shut up, Jaylen — and look up there." Awaiting the boys is an industrial ladder that extends several yards upward. Jaylen lets out a sigh of relief and reaches for the ladder. This climb reminds him of the fire escape from his grandmother's downtown apartment.

After going for about a quarter mile in the darkness, Caleb and Jaylen have eyes on their final escape. They hear a distant banging coming from below.

Caleb's eyes widen in terror. "It's them! It's them! Go." He nervously yanks on Jaylen's pants leg. "Move!" The teens climb faster still, soon reaching the very top. Jaylen quickly unloosens the sewer plate, sliding it off to the side. Caleb and Jaylen climb out of the hole to safety. Together, they set the metal topper back into place.

The teens find themselves in an alley. Jaylen immediately wrinkles up his nose, inhaling a foul odor into his lungs.

"What the hell is that stench??" He looks around the grimy exterior to see baskets of rotten fruit lined up along the wall of the alley. Nearly gagging, his hands rush to cover his nose. Furry rodents leap from basket to basket, enjoying the putrid leftover rot from days prior.

"It's the farmers market…" He surveys the rest of his surroundings. "This alley is gross." Jaylen waits on a response from Caleb – but it doesn't come. Caleb stands atop the sewer plate, lost in thought.

Jaylen tries again. "Caleb, we good?"

"I guess I'm okay," Caleb finally says.

Jaylen buries his nose deep inside his shirt, attempting to stop the nauseating aroma from engulfing him. "Is this going to take long? Because it stinks in this alley…"

"You know what? Forget it." Caleb ventures down the alley, alone.

Already regretting his insensitive words, Jaylen runs to catch up, doing his best at concocting a manufactured version of his feelings. "I'm all ears. What is it?"

"You don't think they killed my dad… Do you?"

Jaylen had never before lied to his best friend, and he wouldn't start today. "I wish I could tell you they did him no harm. But I can't, bro."

"But why would they kill him? He didn't do anything."

"That's the question I've asked myself for years…" Jaylen murmurs. Caleb abruptly stops walking, his eyes boring holes into the brick alley wall.

Jaylen musters up the strength to keep going. He lets his shirt slide back into place, uncovering his nose. "You see, Caleb, they don't give a damn about us. It's time we start to not care about them." This moment establishes a feeling of solidarity between the two, bringing Jaylen a whole new wave of sadness around the meaningless death of his own father.

Caleb turns to his friend. "I can't lose him, Jaylen. He's all I got." He gulps, burying a sob in his throat as he contemplates life without his father, the man who has been his lifelong rock. "Fuck! Fuck!"

"Cal, calm down, bro. Let's lay low for a few hours. Let's hope he's good."

"You're right. Who would have thought you would be calming me down right now?"

Caleb glances up in time to see Jaylen playfully miming a fist toward his gut. They share a lukewarm smile.

All of a sudden, a woman darts through the alley, knocking Jaylen to the ground. She collapses on top of him for a brief moment before scrambling to her feet. "RUN! RUN!" She desperately races up the alley.

"What crawled up her ass and died?" Jaylen gets to his feet, using his hand to try buffing away the nasty dirt and alley grime from his clothing. Before he can catch his breath, two more people scramble their way through the alley, this time sending both Jaylen and Caleb to the ground.

"What the hell is going on?" Caleb asks. The boys roll to safety before being trampled. They watch in shock at the hysteria taking place – countless feet charge madly down the alley.

"What do you think is going on?" Jaylen asks.

The curious teens hop to their feet once it looks safe. Caleb's eyes softly flutter shut, his instincts drawing him inward. He has faced this juncture in his dreams before, but the actuality of it hits him like a ton of bricks. In his mind, he watches as a horde of panicked citizens swarms the congested space. Aging women fall to their knees, incessant prayers escaping their lips, their last hope for repentance. Some of the women get trampled to death by the frenzied onslaught.

Caleb's eyelids peel open, a brave sneer cemented on his face. The ensuing commotion draws him forward to the end of the alley where the clustered mob forms. He marches ahead, landing right into the heart of the chaos.

Jaylen struggles to keep up with Caleb amid the bedlam as he zips in and out between the mob of people. "Cal, slow down, bro. Wait for me."

Military aircrafts overhead circle the immediate area, hoping to manifest themselves as a threat to the potential danger that lies in wait. Police sirens boom, the echoes carrying from one end of the city to the other. Throngs of people, all colors, shapes, and sizes, collide with Caleb's thin frame as he plows ahead into the unknown, wavering not even once.

Jaylen doubles his steps, going as fast as he can to keep up. The skinny teen ahead swerves left, then right, hurdling effortlessly over the multitude of fallen bodies. In trying to keep up with his friend, Jaylen finds himself in the middle of a human cyclone as people scurry every which way. He loses sight of Caleb.

"Caleb, wait! Wait!" Jaylen desperately calls out.

Caleb reaches the end of the gridlocked alley. He comes to a stop, his eyes staring ahead as big as saucers. His heart thumps to a rapid melody of its own, beyond his control.

Jaylen finally comes up behind Caleb, frantically gasping for air. "Oh my God. Oh my God." He leans over, his hands tightly gripping his knees for support. After a few moments of sucking in air like a fish out of water, his posture slowly straightens out. "Jeeeeez, this better be good—"

Frozen side by side, the two boys stare in silent awe at what lies before them. A hellish orange tint illuminates the sky, mingling with a fiery inferno of vibrant red mist as it saturates the airspace. Hundreds of the smaller Akache pods strategically circle through the brilliant highlights of the sky. It's truly a sight to behold — but no one could have expected what was to follow.

Almost as though it was some form of intricate choreography, Akache warriors, male and female, begin free falling from the ships, effortlessly torpedoing like runaway missiles to Earth. Each warrior lands with precision on a single knee. Innocent bystanders cluster in the distance, speechless as they take in the reddish hue of the foreign entities' athletic, toned bodies. Modest cloth scraps of red and black cling from their uniquely shaped exteriors. Their razor-sharp claws grip their weapons. Small children within the crowd hide behind their parents, looking on in fear at the prominent bulging fangs of the Akache warriors. Their oval-shaped faces feature the precise markings of cryptic ancient writing. It's hard to determine the creatures' facial expressions through the markings they wear. Their shoulder blades have less noticeable symbols etched into the skin, just as unrecognizable to the citizens as the facial markings. Each warrior sports a lengthy ponytail extending from the highest point of the head, down to the back. Their distinct almond-shaped eyes are fixated skyward on the blazing red mist. The Akache warriors are each armed with indestructible chest armor, a shield, and a spear-like weapon, each specially constructed entirely out of "anachi," a plentiful natural resource from their home planet.

The spectators still linger, most with wide eyes, unsure what to think of the current goings-on before them. Many choose to fawn over the new galactic arrivals from afar, keeping ample space between them and the invaders, while others venture a few steps closer, pulling out their phones, ready to give the livestream of a lifetime. Aligning with their ceremonial tradition, the Akache warriors rise to both feet in unison. They hoist their spears into the air repeatedly, saluting with triumph, their united voices reciting a chant. Despite being indecipherable to those other than the warriors, the mesmerizing chant of harmonies, as breathtaking as they are daunting, sends a soothing rush of calm over the rowdy citizens.

After some while, the body of each and every warrior gathered confidently rise from the ground. They stand at attention, awaiting their first command from their leader.

In a Jersey accent, a white man wearing a New York Yankees baseball cap yells from the back of the crowd, “Why are you here?” He pushes through the mob, stopping just inches from the Akache warriors. “What do you want? Tell us now.” The red mist dissipates on its own.

“His entitled ass is stupid,” a woman says to the others in the crowd as she backs away. “Look at those spears… This can’t be good.”

Beneath the warriors’ intimidating essence, Caleb finds a morsel of pride in their powerfully unifying stance.

The man in the Yankees cap gets even closer, jabbing his index finger deep into a warrior's chest. "Tell us."

"Aca holoian sol," the Akache warrior replies, sniffing the air surrounding the bothersome man.

"You are in America, pal. We don't speak that here," the man snaps angrily.

Caleb gingerly steps toward the line of warriors, reaching out to the man. "Sir, get away from them."

The man turns his back to the warriors, addressing Caleb. "See, they're harmless. Big, but harmless!"

Lightning cracks through the sky, thunder shakes the earth, and suddenly – the sharp point of a warrior's spear plunges deep into the vile man's back, ripping him in two. Gasps reverberate through the terrified crowd, and within an instant, the gathering becomes a free-for-all as the spectators take off in various directions, screaming and running for their lives.

Chapter 10
Hide and Seek

Swarms of terrified Americans run frenzied through the jammed streets. Bolts of lightning tear through the clouds and into the distinguished city center, igniting storefronts and schools, anything and everything in its path.

The Akache warriors, who have just dropped in to spur mass pandemonium, appear much more sizable than Caleb recalls from his last run-in with them. He becomes overwhelmed by the view, trepidation stirring up deep within his soul. The clan of warriors, hundreds upon hundreds of them, surge through the air with ruthless strength and inconceivable power, annihilating cars, buildings, and fleeing civilians. They target those with the palest skin, violent ambushes coming in fast with a single mighty blow to the victims' skull — instant death.

Near the alley's entrance, Caleb and Jaylen slip in between a dumpster, hoping to stay hidden. They watch as the battle of human versus Akache takes over the streets, converting the upscale neighborhood into one of absolute shambles. The warriors move with agility, challenging gravity as they perform death-defying leaps high into the air.

"Bro, look," Jaylen says, gently poking Caleb in the ribs. "They don't want us. We are not the target." He watches the muscular warriors push aside the African American and Latino citizens from their warpath. Instead, their eyes lock on the white citizens, seeking out the palest ones in the crowd. The brazen warriors lift the people off the ground, viciously flinging them into the air like rag dolls. Suddenly, the Akache pods overhead release countless bronzed spheres the size of basketballs, each one with ancient symbols etched into it. The orbs float ominously above the crowd before extracting the melanin from every person of color within the immediate area. Some try and fail running for cover, while others stand there, helplessly accepting their fate.

Caleb tries some deep breathing to placate himself, but it doesn't help. He and Jaylen watch as the entire area succumbs to chaos.

"Oh, no, my worst fears have come true," Caleb whispers to Jaylen, who keeps his distance while watching the battle as intently as if he were watching his favorite football team demolish its opponents.

"This shit is crazy! Look, Cal, they're massive... Indestructible..." Jaylen's face changes as he realizes the gravity of the situation. He becomes visually shaken, watching the slaughter of the innocent. "Cal… They're relentless and not letting up."

An 80-year-old woman gets hurled several yards toward the boys, landing hard at their feet. Blood coats her frail body, skeletal hands shaking with fear as she reaches out. "Help me. Help us."

Caleb jumps back nervously from the old woman. His mind races, unsure of what he can do to help.

"She's on her own, bro," Jaylen heartlessly says, shrugging.

"No, Jaylen, we got to help her."

"How, bro? This shit is uncontrollable. We don't have a dog in this fight."

"Sure we do."

Caleb steps up and pulls the woman behind the dumpster with Jaylen. Leaning down to comfort her the best he can, the fear in the old lady's eyes consume him. He tries not to tear up as he looks over her blood drenched face. She's unable to move her limbs but she tries nonetheless – and pays the price in unfathomable pain.

"AHHHHH," the woman screams in agony.

Jaylen watches Caleb struggling to roll the elderly woman closer to the dumpster before reluctantly offering up some help. The woman tries smiling at the boys but it hurts too much. She forces her eyes to focus on Caleb and croaks out a few hushed words.

"You remind me of my grandson. He's sixteen. Smart kid, gorgeous blond hair, loves James Baldwin books."

Unsure of where to put his hands, Caleb sets them across the woman's chest. "I'm sorry," he whispers to her.

"I'm afraid to die." Then comes the woman's last request; a simple one. "Don't leave me… Please."

Unable to withstand it, Jaylen turns his back to the scene, releasing himself from watching the inevitable. The elderly woman's eyes slip shut as she drifts away. Choking back a sniffle, Caleb looks to Jaylen for even a thread of pity, any semblance of mercy. Instead, Jaylen stands there, refusing to turn back, his posture cold, unfazed.

In the city center, the terrifying battle rages on with no ending in sight. Now, some of the Akache warriors leap high into the clouds, landing with purpose on the enemy military planes. The armed aircrafts send streams of bullets propelling toward the warriors in victory — but the wasted ammo is all for naught. The warriors' solid physiques effortlessly repel every last bullet that blasts through the sky. Impenetrable protective glass shields the pilots inside each military plane. As though it were nothing, the warriors peel away the glass layer, reach inside, and toss the pilots out into midair, sending them plunging to their deaths.

Lifeless bodies have quickly built up, mounds of them strewn about every inch of the city streets that once buzzed with excitement. Caleb and Jaylen have had enough of the carnage. Seamlessly merging with an escaping mob of terrified Americans, the teens make a run for it. Large clusters of citizens run for several blocks until they make it into the more urban part of town. The swarm begins breaking down into smaller groups, praying for shelter, desperately seeking a moment of peace or an inkling of safety, no matter how brief.

Caleb and Jaylen follow their lead, racing alongside a much smaller cluster of families in search of assistance from anyone who will give it. Darting from apartment building to apartment building, they bang on doors in a frenzy. No luck is to be had… Most buildings have already prepared for this exact moment, prematurely boarding up their windows with sturdy planks of wood.

All of a sudden, a middle-aged white gentleman wearing a KISS t-shirt waves to the tormented crowd. He's joined by his two daughters, eight-year-old twins who clutch tightly onto their dad's shirt. Jaylen eyes him curiously.

"Guys, help me with this door," the man yells. The other side of the glass door is being held shut by an assembly of Black residents who refuse to help their fellow humans. The man screams through the glass. "Open the door! They will kill us!"

Caleb, Jaylen, and the others put their destinationless route on hold and race toward the rundown building. Clusters of people simultaneously grab onto the door handle, yanking hard, finally prying the door open after some time. They all rush inside to safety, they hope.

As the escapees enter, the lingering building residents make a run for their apartments. Doors slam shut one by one, the sound ricocheting through the empty lobby.

"What do we do now?" the man asks as he cradles his two daughters, trying to comfort them the best he can. Without notice, a white woman's bloodied body collides with the glass door, shattering it to pieces. The girls scream, terrified. Caleb and the rest take off, bursting through the emergency exit nearby.

They race up a dark stairwell. Someone in the group yells, "Go! Go!" One of the little girls trip, falling behind her sister. Caleb hurries to grab her up into his arms, not stopping even for a moment. Breathlessly, the group reaches the top, the fifth floor. Now nearly leading the pack, Caleb gently pushes open the door. Finding an empty hallway, the families, Caleb, and Jaylen file out and start aggressively banging on any and all apartment doors.

"Help us!" someone shouts. Another one pipes up. "Let us in! They will kill us!" But no one answers. The man with the twin daughters looks up and down the hallway anxiously. "Why won't someone help us?! Please!"

Jaylen tries kicking in a few of the apartment doors, but he isn't strong enough. "Hello! Open the damn door!" The people huddle closer and closer together as each moment passes. Sounds of bloodshed and destruction from outside the building invade their ears, taunting them. They prepare for the end, bracing themselves both mentally and physically. The diverse group of Americans start to make peace, hugging their family members tight.

"It will be okay, Hillary. Just keep your eyes closed, honey." The man whispers into the ear of one of his daughters, crouching to be at eye level, a lingering feeling of underlying regret in his words.

Caleb and Jaylen rest their backs against the wall, listening as a barrage of screams echo from the floor below. The teens exchange a glance. They know that the chances of outrunning this will be almost impossible. Next comes silence – and then an unsettling chant released by the Akache warriors. They're close, possibly lurking within the dark stairwell from which the group just slipped out. Caleb's eyes stay glued to the door, his heart currently residing in his mouth. A daunting silence lingers. Everyone holds in a breath they feel might be the last. No one moves a muscle, each of them silently praying, wishing, hoping, pleading that the invaders don't find them.

In the distance, a metal bar unbolts. An apartment door at the very end of the hall creaks open ever so slightly. The petrified group instantly races for it, their last chance at possible safety. As soon as the last person gets inside, they bolt up the door, and the men in the group begin pushing heavy pieces of furniture against it.

"That won't be enough," a nervous voice screeches from the back of the room. "They will get through the door!"

"It's all we've got," one of the men replies. "Everybody, stay quiet."

Caleb steps closer to Jaylen and whispers. “Why you so quiet?”

“No reason,” Jaylen whispers back.

“Seems like you’ve changed your tune about things.”

“Nope. I still think they deserve what’s coming to them.”

“You don’t believe that,” Caleb says. Jaylen quickly turns away, leaving his friend wondering whether or not he meant the harsh remark. Caleb looks around the room, searching for answers but finding none. He eyes the group of nervous runaways lining the walls of the tiny apartment. Thick slabs of wood secure the only two visible windows. A few lit candles stand tall on a coffee table in the main living area.

“Whose place is this?” Jaylen asks aloud.

A young woman’s voice lilts in from another room. “Everyone has to eat something,” she says, her tone sweet, yet concerning. She tiptoes into the room with water bottles and sandwiches in hand, casually giving out the refreshments around the room. Shadows within the dimly lit room obscure the woman’s pale face.

Jaylen slits his eyes and taps a finger on his temple. He surveys the twelve or so pale white faces surrounding him. "Ain't this some shit."

"What is it now?" Caleb asks.

"I was just thinking. DuPont Street… It's the street that separates the rich from the poor. One fucking street. Cal, one street over, and you're living high on the hog." Jaylen points an accusing finger at the others in the group. "How can you live in a country where one street separates rich from poor?"

The man from earlier holds onto his daughters even tighter. "Shhh, we don't want trouble. We just want to survive, like you."

"Yeah, sure you do. That's why you are here in our neighborhood. Why not run to your hood? Because you can't – they'll find you there."

Caleb pokes Jaylen in the side, encouraging him to stop spewing these unruly proclamations. "Jaylen, you are going to freak everyone out. Please."

Jaylen completely ignores Caleb. His voice rises in volume, unnerving everyone who's being forced to listen in. "Naw, Caleb. This has got to be said."

"Now, though?"

The young woman steps out from the shadows, getting up in Jaylen's face. "Pipe down before you get all of us killed." For a moment, the glow from the candlelight reveals her face.

"Micky?" Caleb asks, looking wide-eyed at the young woman he and Jaylen met back at Lanier University. It's nice to see a familiar face.

"Caleb?" The two immediately share a hug. Micky has cropped her luxurious locks into a more manageable bob since Caleb last saw her. Her tiny red freckles nearly shimmer in the light.

Caleb turns to Jaylen. "Jaylen, look, it's Micky."

"Whoop-dee-doo. I figured if anyone would be living in the hood, it'd be her. I gave you a little credit for choosing a HBCU… But why live in the hood?"

"I am very much connected to the community here. And yes, I adore the Black community, which is why I chose to attend a HBCU." Micky glances around the room, her eyes searching. "Where's Bree?"

The boys exchange a look but stay quiet. All of a sudden, a powerful vibration moves the floor beneath everyone's feet, interrupting the short-lived reunion between the three. The men jump into action, sprinting across the room, throwing their bodies hard into the bulky furniture stacked against the puny door. Menacing screams emit from the opposite side.

"Everybody, stay quiet," the man with the twins whispers to the others over his shoulder.

"Who in the hell put you in charge?" Jaylen snaps.

"Come on, we are in this together."

"No, false. You are here because your reign as predator number one ran out."

Micky shoves a bottle of water into Jaylen's hand as an attempt to cool him down. "Guys, we've got to work together or else none of us will make it."

"I beg to differ. Those things aren't after us," Jaylen says, motioning to himself and the other three Black people present in the room."

"What is he talking about?" Micky asks, her eyes shifting to Caleb.

Caleb clears his throat before answering, trying to buy himself a little more time. "They're called 'Akache.' They are only after certain Americans…" He gives a pointed look to the white people in the group.

Micky struggles to piece together Caleb's hints. A few moments later, her eyebrows lift in shock. "You're lying."

"No, we are not."

"They were building an army," Jaylen adds.

"So, they want to kill white people? Why?" Micky asks, confused.

Jaylen swallows his instinct to blurt out his rage and instead raises his hand as if he's in school. "Because everything the white man touches dies — the wars, poverty, devastation around the world. Look around at this gentrification, Becky. Systematic racism at its finest."

Micky takes a deep breath, restraining herself from denying Jaylen's blatant accusations against the entire white race. "I hear you, Jaylen. But this is different."

"How is it different? Because you are the hunted now?"

"I, like most people, are sorry for the past, but we've got to move into the future."

"How, Micky? You won't let us."

A middle-aged white woman with dark bouncy hair steps out into the light. "Yes, my ancestors caused some pain, but we aren't them!"

"But you benefit from it," Jaylen retorts. "And you say nothing."

The white citizens in the room listen with rapt attention, their current dire situation forgotten for the moment. They watch the impassioned debate going on between Jaylen and Micky, their eyes darting back and forth to keep up.

"You know what," Jaylen begins, "how about we end it all right now?" Caleb grabs Jaylen, holding him back. He feels his muscles tense under his grip.

"What are you going to do?" Caleb snarls in his ear.

"It's not what I'm going to do…" He breaks free from Caleb's grip, running across the room to the apartment door. "We are in here! We are in here!" The horrified citizens gasp in shock at Jaylen's life-threatening action — life-threatening for them, anyway…

"Are you crazy?!" The man with twins says, sending Jaylen clear across the room with a forceful push. Jaylen comes creeping back over, a pushing match ready to ensue. Caleb runs to the middle of the room, holding steadfast in his attempt to calm down both parties. But it's too late. Loud thumping crashes against the door, the intensity shaking the furniture, their time of safety wearing incredibly thin.

"They found us."

Chapter 11
The Race to Light

A few minutes have passed since the shoving match first broke out between Jaylen and the rest of the weary escapees. One of the men springs from amid the frightened group and manages to restrain the cocky teen, wrapping his arms around him, pinning him to the wall. The violent thrashing against the door is relentless. Everyone trapped inside the apartment makes the best of the limited space, huddling together, an onslaught of bodies shrouding Jaylen, trying to keep him quiet as he wriggles with contempt.

"Let me go," Jaylen argues, his words muffled.

"Shhhh, they will hear us," Micky warns. The uneasy group stares at the door with panic-stricken eyes, wishing for the banging to stop.

But Jaylen keeps it up, causing Caleb to do the unthinkable. He roughly clasps a hand around his friend's mouth, putting a stop to the insolent ranting. "Sorry, buddy."

Jaylen tries wriggling free with a vengeance, but the diverse group has had more than enough by now. They squeeze tighter the harder he flails about, trying to help restrict further movement. Micky jumps into the middle of the action, taking over guarding duties. She switches places with Caleb, securing Jaylen's mouth with an equal amount of intensity, if not more.

Once released from his spot within the nervous cluster, Caleb stands tall and quietly slinks his way toward the apartment door. He glances back to steal a peek at the distressed group, their faces stricken with a mixture of anxiety and fear. Caleb forges ahead, moving with the precision of one trying to avoid the extremity-losing threat of a laser beam security system. With each careful step comes an even deeper breath than the last. As his Nikes drag across the aged wooden floorboards, they release a sharp squeak, startling him like never before.

The harsh thumping on the door comes to an abrupt stop. Caleb doesn't move a muscle, staring terrified at the blockade of vintage furniture separating him from the danger that lurks, lying in wait just outside the door. His feet gingerly lift from the floor. All the while, the teen maintains an even stance, his eyes locking steadfast on the door.

"They're outside the door," Caleb quietly whispers to the troubled group behind him. "I feel them." Still actively being pinned to the wall by the desperate cluster, Jaylen squirms with the most vigor yet, doing his best to make their location known to whatever it is that stands on the opposite side of the apartment's flimsy construction. Caleb holds his index finger in midair, and everyone on edge nearly forgets to breathe.

One of the twin girls releases a sneeze just then, cutting the dead silence of the room like the startling explosion of a bomb. Everyone in the group shoots dirty looks at the noise culprit, making the little girl tear up. The man picks up his daughter and she buries her face into his chest, sniffling. "Shhh, honey, it's okay," the man whispers, comforting her.

Caleb swiftly turns back to face the group. "They're gone." He releases a heavy sigh, followed by everyone else in the room. As things wind down, Jaylen roughly pushes away the two men holding the bulk of him.

"Get the hell off me," Jaylen explodes.

"We are only trying to save lives," one of the men explains.

"Wrong! You're trying to save y'all lives. Caleb, what's up, man… This how you do me?"

Caleb turns to Jaylen, puffing out a breath of air. "I had no choice. There are kids in here."

"So?!" Jaylen squints at Caleb, a disgusted look on his face.

Micky wanders over to play peacemaker. "Cool it, Jaylen. I have some cold beer in the fridge— "

"I don't drink beer. Why would you assume that?"

"I didn't. I just wanted you to take the edge off."

"Whatever. I'm leaving here, even if I have to fight everybody in this room." Jaylen's just about to stomp off, but Caleb grabs his arm, pushing him through the swinging doors of the kitchen.

It's just the two of them in the kitchen. Finally, they have a chance to breathe.

"You are out of line, Jaylen!"

"So what, Caleb?!" Jaylen throws a fit like a ten-year-old. He hefts himself up onto the counter, moping, his legs swinging gently. He seethes inside at the idea of telling his friend where to go. But Caleb reaches out and palms Jaylen's face like a basketball, pulling him closer.

"Bro, we in this together," Caleb says calmly while he and Jaylen are eye to eye. "Wishing death on them won't bring life to us. We will get through this." He takes a deep breath as though attempting to exhale all of his inner turmoil. "I just need my friend. My boy. Maybe it's too late and you're long gone."

Finally, Caleb pulls back. Defeated, he sits down at the kitchen table, his shoulders slumping deeper into the inescapable abyss of sorrow. A few moments pass before Jaylen pokes out his lower lip, pouting like a child who knows they've done wrong.

"But y'all didn't have to hold me like that. You knew I wasn't going to open that door."

"Yeah, I knew, but they didn't.

Micky nudges open the door, poking her head in. "Are we good, boys?"

Jaylen's head whips toward the door. "Who you calling a 'boy'?" He turns back to Caleb. "You see? Racial…"

Caleb concedes, nodding to keep Jaylen pacified. "We are good, Micky. Thanks." Micky nods and returns to the main living area. Soon after, the only other African Americans in the group, a couple in their twenties, join Caleb and Jaylen in the kitchen. Jaylen immediately admires the woman's busty cleavage, meditating on a passionate lust-filled fantasy as he shifts awkwardly on the counter. The young woman takes a seat at the kitchen table. She moves her freshly braided locks from her face. Her figure is the kind that most guys would mortgage a house over. Jaylen allows himself to temporarily sideline the anger for his cause.

"I'm Trina," the woman says.

"I'm Caleb, and this is Jaylen." Caleb motions to his pouty friend.

Trina continues. "This is Evan, my boyfriend."

"Boyfriend?" Jaylen comments, a repulsed smirk on his face.

Evan stands at six feet, is well-spoken, and maintains the immaculate physique of a bodybuilder. "I'm Evan. Good to meet you both."

"Yeah, yeah, sure," Jaylen grumbles.

Evan pushes the kitchen door open just slightly, taking in a brief overview of the others present across the apartment. He then wanders over to the table, joining Trina in a chat with the boys, his words both deliberate and emotional.

"I have thought long and hard about this," Evan begins with a trace of hesitation buried in his otherwise soothing voice. "I'm joining Akache."

"Me too," Trina says, gripping Evan's forearm excitedly as if they had just announced their engagement.

This unexpected proclamation from the strangers forces Caleb upright in his seat, barely able to contain himself. “But why?” He looks on, horrified.

“Why not? The commander is right. The things he said during his livestream are facts.”

Jaylen victoriously jumps down from the counter, playfully jabbing Caleb with his elbow. He is simply thrilled by the couple’s revelation. “See, Caleb?! I’m not the crazy one after all.”

Caleb puts a hand in the air to stifle Jaylen’s elbow jabs. “I never said you were crazy. I just wanted you to think about it.”

“What is there to think about? We’ll be indestructible.” Jaylen’s clearly getting carried away too soon as usual. “I wonder if we get to create our own Akache names,” he thinks aloud.

Caleb turns to the couple, casting a gravely displeased look their way. “But… People are dead. And if you join Akache, you too will have blood on your hands.”

Evan does his best to keep his voice down, but Jaylen’s excitement easily revs him up. “I’m with Jaylen. I mean, what do we have to lose?”

“Everything! The soul of who you are… Just listen to yourselves.”

“Caleb, I think you are trying to talk sense into the wrong race of people,” Trina says, motioning to the door, back to where the others remain gathered. "Look at them out there. No, really look at them."

Rising to his feet, Caleb nudges open the kitchen door, peering out into the living room at the group of innocent people hoping to survive, trying their best to wait out the storm together. "I see a father comforting his kids."

Trina slithers up behind Caleb, the words that follow pulling at his fragile heartstrings. "Now, imagine if they were black. Who would care? Hell, the government sent one million of us in order to save their lives. Fuck that! It's payback time."

"No," Caleb resists, "it would make us no better than they are."

"You're saying that because you're sitting here and not in there, Caleb." Trina returns to the kitchen table, her hands clasping together triumphantly. Her position on the matter at hand is set in stone, and Caleb swallows her brutal analysis like a handful of nails.

"I truly understand each of your points, but I can't help thinking why. Why would Akache not use them as a resource, collateral or something? The act alone is questionable. Something just doesn't add up for me."

On the other side of the door, Micky stands, overhearing every word of the conversation. She's unable to hold her tongue, so she barges in. "I'm sorry, I know that I'm probably the last person you want giving you advice. But you are all making a big mistake if you join Akache."

As a way of expressing their decision on the matter, Jaylen, Evan, and Trina gather one by one on the opposite side of the table. The three enact a steady gaze toward Caleb, their judging eyes awaiting his verdict.

Micky takes a step toward Caleb, requesting his attention. "Caleb, before you make your decision, think about your community. Since moving here, I now fully understand that the African American experience is diverse in ideology. The heritage is rich with love and prolific in profound awareness. I want to learn more and be a better ally. Don't make me do it alone." The end of Micky's appeal exudes pain from the very depths of her soul. Even Jaylen looks touched by the feeling in Micky's delivery, allowing himself the tiniest bit of wiggle room on his decision for the moment, but he stays where he is.

"Micky, I want to believe you, God knows I do," Caleb says. "But America has continually shown us her true colors, and this time, I'm believing who she has shown us to be."

Micky gives up on Caleb, notes her lack of progress with Jaylen, and instead turns to Evan and Trina last. "And you two—"

"We've made up our minds," Evan replies abruptly before ushering Trina back into the living room. They disappear behind the swinging door. Not a moment later… "Guys, come in here!" Evan yells out.

Caleb, Jaylen, and Micky rush out of the kitchen to see what else could possibly be wrong. As soon as the three enter, Caleb notices that the furniture has been removed from the door – and the room is empty.

Instantly, Jaylen rages. "See! Selfish bastards!" He roughly tosses aside an end table from out of his path and sprints through the apartment door.

"Jaylen, wait," Micky calls, shrugging on her jacket. "I'm coming with you." Caleb rushes to catch up with the both of them.

Finally, free from the apartment, Caleb, Jaylen, and Micky run through the dark hallway. A partially shattered window sits at the end of the hall. Jaylen quickly breaks away the remaining glass using his elbow.

Outside, the sky above wears the hue of a devilish red. Thin blueish lines of smoke frame the outer perimeter. Determined to contain the burgeoning anarchy, a host of military tanks rolls up and down the street with urgency. Meanwhile, the Akache warriors are still at it, running rampant, effortlessly flinging countless spectators one by one to their harrowing demise.

Five stories high into the air, Jaylen lands onto the fire escape, racing down to ground level at shocking speed. Micky and Caleb follow behind, unable to match neither his cat-like moves nor impressive pace. Jaylen locks his eyes intently on the multitude of defenders who fight back the Akache with brute force.

"Follow me," Jaylen says.

Once the last pair of feet touch down at the bottom, the trio silently agrees that the safer option is to settle within the mayhem — with so much going on around them, they're more likely to slip right past any immediate threats. Running parallel to one another, the three friends scurry up the bustling street, leaping over dead body after dead body every step of the way.

They pass by a cluster of Black gang members. The hulking men gather around a blinged-out car, having an intense deliberation on whether or not to join the fight with Akache. Some shove each other back and forth, screaming obscenities in disagreement. Others commit to what they feel is their obligation, launching themselves from the front of the car, toward the blinding light of the Akache. They surrender themselves, arms lifting as an invisible force guides them deeper into the mysterious glow. The gang members reluctant to join their buddies waste no time sticking around. They immediately get swept up with the mob of Americans racing forth to escape the pockets of spellbinding light.

Caleb, Jaylen, and Micky continue their journey across the chaotic street, dodging in and out of oncoming traffic as Americans run amok. On the west corner stands a prominent church building, complete with stained glass. Black churchgoers emerge from their place of worship, searching for a direct route to safety, but there isn't one. With nowhere left to go, a large portion of them fall to the ground, kneeling in unison, incessantly reciting the Lord's Prayer. Other churchgoers burst out into song, attempting to keep spirits high. The melodious harmonies blend together, forcing Caleb's pace to come to a near complete stop. He watches as the churchgoers suddenly rise to their feet, heart-wrenching tears streaming down their beautiful brown faces. Then finally, their arms lift in reverence — to the massive Akache ship hovering immediately overhead.

"You are our God now. Yield us Your freedom, Lord," the worshippers chant in succession. Gradually, the feet of every last one separates from the soil, and they begin their ascent into the enchanting illumination, the light of which reminds them of God calling them home. Each of their chocolate bodies, once enveloped in the hypnotic brilliance, rotates in midair as the blinding glow eats away at the rich, creamy melanin of their skin.

Micky's eyes fill with tears as she stares up at the sky, mesmerized by the angelic moment taking place right before her.

"Guys, we have to keep moving," Caleb urges, heading straight into the cyclone of people. Micky rejoins, barely missing a step. The teens cut through a recreational park a bit further up the street. Athletically fit, tall Black men shoot hoops on the local basketball court. Sure enough, as the Akache ship approaches, the players put their game on hold, instantly racing to the edge of the fence, peeking through the gaps for a closer look. They stare with extreme shock and curiosity as more and more bodies ascend into the belly of the overbearing spacecraft. Caleb watches the men from afar, feeling a temporary wave of helplessness. Deep down, he knows that before long, the entire Black population will be taken in by the Akache – if he doesn't try to change things, that is.

The teens watch as the Black citizens soar into the persuasive white light. A single basketball plummets to the ground, left behind. Soon, they realize that the faster the Black citizens enter the ship, the faster they are transformed into fighting Akache warriors. All of a sudden, Jaylen makes up his mind… Without any warning at all, he races toward the light, leaping into the radiant blaze with his arms open wide, gladly accepting what is to come. The courageous teen rises skyward, floating into his destiny without a fear or a care in the world.

"No, Jaylen, no!" Caleb screams up at his best friend.

Chapter 12
The First Blow

It's getting late in the afternoon. As strong as ever, the unprecedented battle rages on and on between America and its galactic invaders, the Akache. Many American cities across the globe have since been ransacked to the point of near obliteration, thanks to the invasion of countless brooding Akache warriors. Every major airport overflows with citizens desperate to escape the repulsive attacks from the Akache regime — but this attempt proves to be futile. Government agencies have simultaneously enacted a ban to halt all air travel, sparking a slew of traffic jams all over the country as citizens madly seek other forms of escape.

Roughly sixty miles north of Washington, D.C., near Camp David, the President and his family are safely tucked away in a heavily guarded, secure bunker. President Reid sits in his temporary Situation Room several miles under the Catoctin Mountains. He's on the phone, making call after call, seeking emergency deployment support from all across the globe.

Just outside the door, a swarm of armed Secret Service agents line the wall. They patrol the entire perimeter of the bunker. Utilizing only the most advanced tech, the agents have satellites surveying every square inch of the grounds, ensuring the President's safety.

Back inside the Situation Room, President Reid speaks in his usual boisterous tone with foreign leaders across the pond. Every last one of these foreign countries has idly stood by while witnessing the torturous annihilation America's been forced to withstand. Surely, they each express their sympathy toward the situation, but not one of them is willing to risk their own military for support in an unbeatable battle like this one. The President cordially accepts each statement of consolation, along with each rejection of support. Annoyance shows on his face as he becomes more and more flustered by the other countries' intense unwillingness to assist his cause. The President looks around, taking in the makeshift Situation Room. It's much smaller than the real one, able to comfortably fit only six people at once. The claustrophobic feel of the room is heightened by the lack of windows, toying with the President's anxiety now and then. In fact, he's already popped several Xanax in the last hour alone as an attempt to calm his nerves. A brisk knock at the door comes as a welcome excuse to put his unpleasant cold-calls on hold.

"Come on in," President Reid says. The door swings open. In walks three Cabinet members — two men and one woman. The trio saunter into the room, each of them wearing their own grim expression. They take a seat at the small table, set their briefcases on the floor, and roll up their sleeves; it's clear they mean business. Although eager to get started, they do their best to tread lightly and patiently wait for Molly, the Chief of Staff, to enter, popping in just long enough to set plastic-wrapped intelligence briefings on the table in front of each of them. She exits the room, securing the door behind her. One of the Cabinet members immediately turns on a nearby television — the only one available in this underground facility.

On the screen, intense video footage of Akache warriors plays as they savagely attack countless American citizens across various cities and states. The next clip shows a field of bronzed spheres with unintelligible symbols floating overhead, orbiting the gloomy nighttime sky. These metallic orbs cast peaceful white rays over the immediate populace. One by one, each Black citizen unfortunate enough to be experiencing this nightmare gets their melanin ripped away.

President Reid watches this heinous turn of events in horror, a hand clasped to his mouth. He nearly gags as he attempts to come to terms with this new reality. The sight of such torturous acts being performed on innocent people propels the President out of his chair. He paces the limited span of the room, trying to look away, his eyes always being drawn back toward the carnage on the screen.

"Turn it off. NOW!" President Reid shouts. The female Cabinet member heeds to the President's wishes, quickly grabbing the remote to mute the volume. Realizing that nearly anything they could say might be seen as irrelevant and trivial, the three remain silent for the time being. They watch the President as he paces the airless Situation Room, waiting for him to be the first to speak.

"How many are dead?" President Reid demands to know. The President's tone catches the woman off-guard, and she lets out a quiet gulp as she opens her file and rifles through her papers for any possible answers.

"There is no way of knowing," the woman states. "Maybe five thousand thus far."

"I need an accurate number."

"Sure, Mr. President. With all due respect, sir, this could be catastrophic on all accounts."

"How do we stop them?" President Reid asks regretfully, already aware that his team hasn't the slightest clue. The Cabinet members hesitate, exchanging glances, each waiting for the other to answer. President Reid nods expectantly; just as he thought. He rests his back up against the wall. "You three are the most important people in my Cabinet," he starts. "We need a plausible strategy that will save lives— "

A sudden knock on the door interrupts that thought. "Come in," President Reid briskly calls, a mere hint of frustration in his tone. Homeland Security Advisor Brad Doley stands in the doorway. He wears street clothes and a baseball cap. The President casts a judging eye over his too casually dressed advisor.

"I got here as fast as I could," Doley sputters. "It's not looking good, Mr. President. Our intelligence has confirmed that there is a second mothership somewhere in the Midwest, several miles from Detroit."

The President slits his eyes at this newly acquired info. "Why Detroit? There is nothing there. Abandoned establishments… A declining city and population…"

"You are missing the point, Mr. President. This is about building the biggest army possible. They live in Detroit."

"They?"

"Yes, they," Doley affirms, his meaty finger pointing directly at the television. On the screen, some Black Americans in the crowd excitedly cheer on the violence afflicting their pale fellow citizens, while others frown upon the senseless acts of savagery caused by the hand of the Akache. Doley continues. "They are joining Akache at an alarming rate. We won't be able to compete with them." President Reid rushes over to the table and pulls away the plastic from his intelligence briefing packet. "That's exactly what they want."

"Maybe we can offer a stimulus or reparations to these people if they decide to stay with the United States," the President rambles.

The solitary female Cabinet member at the table keeps her eyes glued to the unfolding news on-screen. She pulls herself away from the grim images long enough to school President Reid, giving him a discouraging but true account of life for many in the States. She begins.

"Mr. President, let's be honest here. Why would Black Americans, at this point, side with the United States? Look at our economic structure; it's not benefiting them. They don't have a stake in this. Akache has given them a voice, a voice like they've never seen before. For over four hundred years, they've asked, pleaded, and begged for the union to consider legislation in an effort to elevate their communities."

A note of tension catches in the frustrated woman's voice. She pauses, taking a breath and raking her hand through her abundantly luscious dark mane. Her eyes focus back onto the screen, her head shaking as she comes to terms with what's occurring on the screen.

"Can we even blame them for joining the Akache regime? Are they insurrectionists? Are they traitors? I think history will be the judge, considering what they have gone through," the woman says, pleased with herself as she wraps up her informed sentiment in favor of the Black Americans and their current plight. She comfortably sinks back into her chair as though an unbearable weight had been lifted from her shoulders. Doley, however, sees things quite differently. He cozies up to the woman, getting right up in her space, his loathsome blubber belly rubbing up against her back.

"Your points are valid," Doley starts. "But when you take that pledge of allegiance to that flag, you promise your loyalty."

The woman barks back. "Why should they live up to their end of the bargain when we haven't, Advisor Doley?"

President Reid rejoins his dueling staff at the table, his index fingers carefully caressing his bottom lip in thought. "So, Doley, what are our options?" Doley looks to the President as he reveals a pack of cigarettes, Salem Menthol Lights, from his pocket. The President nods, giving him permission to smoke due to the circumstances. Relieved, Doley lights up, happily inhaling the deadly nicotine deep into his lungs.

"We take out the mothership and we get rid of these bastards."

"And how do you suppose we do that?"

"There's only one way, Mr. President – nuclear."

"Are you out of your mind? There will be mass deaths in the tens of millions!"

"Yes, that's collateral damage," Doley says. "It's the price you pay to go to war."

"No. We can't." President Reid puts his foot down on Doley's vile plan.

"We must, if we hope to have a chance at preserving what our founders deemed as the 'American way.'"

The President ruminates on Doley's chilling prognosis. "What if the nukes do nothing? What if it's like air to them?"

Doley shrugs. "Then we go to plan B."

"What's plan B?"

"I'm working on that now."

From an overhead speaker, Chief of Staff Molly's voice booms, stumbling through her rapid-fire words with just a touch of underlying anguish. "Mr. President, switching to an alternate satellite – please look at the screen."

The Cabinet members anxiously swivel around in their chairs for a better look at the footage, hoping for the best but expecting the worst. Everyone focuses intently as they watch the following clip of Akache's mothership levitating not more than a quarter mile from the White House.

"What do you think they're doing, Doley?" President Reid asks, concerned. Doley rises, stepping closer and closer to the television for a better look. Having forgotten his glasses back at the office, he doesn't stop inching ahead until he's standing immediately in front of the screen, squinting.

"Mr. President, look at where the main ship is positioned as compared to the smaller ships…"

"Cut to the chase, Doley," President Reid snaps. "What are you saying?"

Doley mindlessly extends his index finger, marking up the digitally enhanced television screen as if solving an equation in math class. "I'm saying they're bluffing. The ships are staged to intimidate, but they are teasing our response."

"That's it, Doley?"

"Yes. Sir, I've counteracted a numerous amount of deadly missions just by enacting that tactic when I was in the military."

"I trust your word on that, but I have my doubts."

"Have we tried contacting them?"

"By all means, sir, but it's not that easy. We don't have a phone number for them, Mr. President." The hint of sarcasm in Doley's words helps ease the tension in the room. "But the military is at full force and ready at your command."

Suddenly the footage on the television fizzles out to nothing but a black screen — and then filled by the face of Commander Karnitu. He sits on a red metallic throne, his long red ponytail now braided all the way down his back. Foreign symbols cover the commander's face, unintelligible to the human onlookers' naked eyes. The metal red hue of his skin glistens under the blaring lights of the invading ships. Karnitu has a male surrogate in his clutches, squeezing with zero remorse for the pain he's causing the poor human soul under his power.

Everyone in the makeshift Situation Room hops to their feet and inches closer to the television, quickly getting drawn in. They cast their inward judgments, deeming Karnitu a 'monster' and a 'threat' to democracy all over the world. On the screen, the surrogate tries to relax his body, allowing the commander's menacing warning to be articulated through his lips.

"Greetings from Akache, the reign of Ahku. Our mothership, the guiding light into the darkened abyss abounds. Time has held its value beyond your planet's existence. The Akache have exposed your planet's sinuous goal of colonization — it's flawed, to say the least. One million Belivians weren't enough to rid your country of its atrocities. A debilitating stench inhibits those of the Belivian race that remain. They belong to Akache, and we demand they be freed."

"This motherfucker is a crazy weirdo," Doley exclaims to no one in particular. He turns to President Reid. "This is why you never negotiate with terrorists, Mr. President."

"Shhh, maybe there's more," the President murmurs.

The commander resumes his monologue with the help of his surrogate's voice box. "The Belivian gene that my brethren have flowing through their veins is enough to awaken a billion planets. You have suppressed their need to be free long enough. I would imagine the freedom the Belivians seek dares to threaten your existence as an oppressor. Ceasing the strong depth and rich lineage of Belivians was never going to last—"

Karnitu's surrogate suddenly breaks free from the trance and realizes the current state he's in. He feels the commander's talons wrapped tightly around his neck. "Please, let go! I can't breathe."

The evil commander ignores the man's desperate plea for air and instead squeezes more tightly than ever before, reveling with euphoria at the surrogate's mounting pain. Then for a moment, Karnitu smiles, exposing his perfectly straight, razor-sharp fangs, much to the horror of the viewers standing right in front of the television screen. Tossing the ailing man as if it were nothing, the commander instantly finds another surrogate to finish off his speech. He grips the other poor surrogate by the neck and continues on.

"How much longer will my Belivian brothers and sisters be dominated by the means of an inferior plight? I am here to say, 'no more.' NO MORE."

The next moment, Karnitu's image on the screen is replaced by a barrage of video clips from just the last ten decades. Footage of African Americans getting beaten, lynched, and handcuffed by police officers fills the screen.

"Is this being played for the world to see?" President Reid asks Doley.

"Yes." Doley confirms his statement, showing the livestream playing from his smartphone. "Can you demand all networks stop the feed?"

The President pauses in thought for a moment, mulling over Doley's suggestion before pivoting back to his initial thought. "No. The world has a right to hear and see this."

"But this will certainly hamper race relations, Mr. President."

"Watching those horrifying images, I gather it's too late for that." The government officials continue watching the atrocious footage, a sickening feeling settling in their stomach.

Karnitu takes over the screen once again. "Reid, relinquish what is not yours. You don't have the capacity to preserve the strength that you're withholding."

Doley swiftly turns to the President, confused. "Mr. President, what is he talking about?"

President Reid hesitates, stumbling over his words. "He's talking about the Belivians – Black people."

"You don't seem so sure about that."

"I'm positive it's what they want," the President states. Doley takes this in and nods slowly, making a mental note in his head.

On the screen, Karnitu squeezes his current surrogate one last time, prompting his voice to shift into the most forbidding tone imaginable. "Those images were my peoples' pain for far too long. The day of reckoning is here."

The government officials hold their breath, waiting for the monstrous commander to continue – but he doesn't.

All of a sudden, on the screen, the metallic spacecraft encompassing a majority of the sky splits open wide. The thick, enormous metal paneling separates, harshly spewing out a mysterious red mist from amid the opening. Finally, Karnitu makes his reappearance – he glides out from the towering ship overhead, flanked by a few hundred Akache warriors armed with their signature weapons, including indestructible chest armor, shields, and spear-like weapons.

Forceful winds come out of nowhere, guiding the fearsome commander from the mouth of the ship, down to Pennsylvania Avenue. Coming to a stop, the commander hovers just several yards away from the White House, ready to do his worst. Karnitu lifts his hands to the sky, shooting powerful bolts of lightning from his peculiarly elongated fingertips.

The luscious green landscape surrounding the White House sinks deeper into the ground, creating an enriched ditch. A wind gust bursts forth, shaking the historical building. One by one, each and every window shatters to bits. Sections of the roof are completely demolished. The protective fencing securing the perimeter gets caught up in the terrifying gale, openly exposing the monumental architecture to the public for the first time.

Again, Karnitu hoists his arms — this time, even higher into the sky, summoning the power of the galactic gods. This brings forth a massive cloud of dark, smoldering smoke, which encapsulates the glorified

Akache commander. His chants come quietly but no less chilling.

Down below, the White House has been nearly obliterated. Its constructed remains separate from the ground, lifting thousands of feet into the air by the force of an unearthly tempest.

The President of the United States crowds around the television with his staff, each one of them doing their very best to stay strong and mask their grave disdain for the terrifying goings-on they're witnessing. Time almost seems to stop, with each passing second creeping along slower and slower.

Back on the screen, they watch as Karnitu finally surrenders his arms to his side, commanding the White House to plunge back into the Earth's soil. The once monumental icon of history smashes into countless pieces. As the dust settles, Karnitu makes his proclamation with a threatening fist held to the sky. "I will ask no longer; it's time we take what's rightfully ours."

Chapter 13
Race and Guns

An assemblage of shrieks and wails pierce through the sound barrier, rising high above the mesmerizingly chilling harmony of the Akache chant. From overhead, a blazing white spear of light shoots down toward the Earth like a fireball. Jaylen has officially cemented his decision to join the Akache regime by ascending into the ethers with his fellow citizens. His lanky body twists and turns amid the fine siphon of light. The paralyzing trance being transmitted by the Akache's spacecraft hasn't yet fully taken hold of Jaylen's consciousness. Staring helplessly, he watches hundreds of African Americans float like zombies, getting pulled closer and closer to the opening of the ship. Jaylen struggles to get out any words, suddenly feeling his inner soul being yanked in all directions.

"What am I doing?" he manages to say while being sucked upward into the depths of the unknown. Then it happens… Chunks of melanin from his body begin dissolving right before his eyes, leaving behind glaringly pasty patches on both his arms and legs. An unpleasant burning sensation singes over the now pale blotches of skin.

The sensation jolts him awake, returning his consciousness to reality. For an instant, his mind flashes to memories of the grandmother he's on the path to leaving behind. Fragmented doubt creeps into his decision of becoming one with the encroaching regime. "I've changed my mind. I don't want to be Akache. Let me down. Let me down!"

On the ground below, Caleb and Micky watch, trying to keep their eyes on Jaylen as his body whirls within the human cyclone. They are clueless to the fact that their friend has changed his mind.

"Let me down," Jaylen screams again with as much power as he can muster. All of a sudden, the rapid movement of his body halts. Frozen, he dangles in midair for a long moment – and then plummets to the ground at a dangerous speed.

From below, Caleb notices his friend's gangly form rapidly approaching from its sky-high starting point, and urgently jumps into action. He rounds up as many willing bystanders as possible, and together, the diverse group of citizens huddle together. As Jaylen's body descends from overhead at a breakneck speed, the citizens below give it all they have, helping to soften the blow of the teen's harsh landing. He thuds to the ground, colliding with the spectators, sending them all tumbling like dominoes. Jaylen acts fast, tucking and rolling along the coarse pavement. His body comes to a stop but doesn't budge; he's out cold.

Caleb and Micky fight through the unruly swarm to get to their friend. They race over and crouch beside his lifeless body. Micky looks on in fear, but Caleb reaches out, gently slapping the sensitive skin of Jaylen's face. Jaylen begins to groan, still unmoving. A woman steps out from the crowd, veering over to where Jaylen lies — and empties her entire water bottle right in his face.

Jaylen immediately hops to his feet, wide awake, shivering, and shaking the water from his clothes. "Where am I?!" he shrieks. Simultaneously a mob of Akache warriors marches toward the herd. Caleb and Micky usher Jaylen to safety, pulling him from off the street, to underneath an awning. The teens sit, nervously huddled together. Jaylen attempts to silence his jitters caused by the recent trauma.

"Jaylen, are you okay? What happened?" Caleb asks.

"I don't know… I was in the light. Then darkness happened."

"What do you mean darkness?" Micky says with sarcasm flowing from her words. Glancing over her shoulder, Micky splits her focus, tending to Jaylen while keeping an eye out for any possible dangers that may be lurking from behind.

"I mean what I said. I got scared, alright?" Jaylen hangs his head. Caleb puts a hand on his friend's shoulder.

"It's okay, Jay. You are okay now," Caleb reassures him. Pondering, Caleb squints in thought. "So, the light just dropped you? But no one else is falling… Why you?" He cautiously gets to his feet, watching from afar as the overhead spacecraft hungrily devours countless bodies of African American citizens. "The last time I checked, you weren't white. Why would it release you?" Caleb continues questioning.

With defiance, Jaylen pushes Caleb aside. "Because I changed my mind, okay? I told them I didn't want to go."

Caleb can't tear his eyes away, his intense stare locked on the Akache army as they take no prisoners, swallowing whole bodies in midair. He starts to overthink. "No, Jaylen, you made a choice. Most of the people taken by the ships haven't made a choice — the government made it for them out of fear."

"Caleb, what are you talking about now?"

"This is ultimately about choice."

"So?"

"So, most of them aren't making a choice; they're acting on the choice that has been made for them." Caleb turns around to see Micky tapping on his shoulder with urgency.

"Guys, we got to go," Micky says, slowly backing away from the street. "Look!" The boys turn to see a horrifying vision… Thousands of Akache warriors fill the sky. As if on cue, they nosedive in succession from their hovering pods to the ground, preparing for yet another battle.

"Shit," Caleb starts, "there's a million of them."

The three friends frantically charge up the street, stopping only once reaching the massive structure of the rundown Genesee Mall. Abandoned for almost ten years, protective bars line the mall's windows and doors, an attempt to deter and ultimately keep out any and all trespassers. Mother Nature has since established a lush home within the building. Weeds and vines trail along, canopying the disheveled exterior of the infrastructure and efficiently obscuring its appearance. Micky catches sight of two women as they cut through an alley leading to the well-hidden back entrance of the mall. They enter one of the back doors.

"Look," Micky says, poking Caleb in the ribs. "Where are they going?" The teens hurry to keep their sight on the women and follow after them, leaving ample space between. No one is to be trusted at this moment. They gingerly creep over to another door at the rear of the building. Caleb and Jaylen combine their strength to pry off the wooden boards that cover the doors. They work as quickly as possible, fearful of the swarm of others coming up right behind them.

Finally, they break through. Caleb pushes everyone into the dark lobby just in time. He sneaks a peek outside as hundreds of terrified citizens rush past the door not a moment too soon. The teens heave sighs of relief, but it isn't over yet; they have to keep moving. They spot a stairwell leading downstairs and head for it. Once inside, the darkness is so thick that they can't even see their hands in front of their faces. Caleb reaches out for Jaylen and Micky.

"Hold onto me. I'll guide us down."

"I guess this is the meaning of the blind leading the blind," Jaylen replies with a chuckle. Once the teens reach the bottom, they come face to face with a door.

"Shhhhh," Caleb warns. With the utmost caution, he turns the knob and nudges the door open an inch or two. He first notices several halls leading in opposite directions, and then spots the two women from earlier walking further along the corridor ahead of them. Caleb quietly tiptoes out to follow them, urging his friends forward. "Guys, stay close."

As they slip out from the stairwell, the movement stirs up a cloud of dust, provoking a coughing fit from Jaylen.

"Shhhh," Micky sharply reprimands.

"Girl, back off of me. This dust is killing my allergies," Jaylen replies. Micky rolls her eyes at his remark and continues walking. Caleb leads them down the corridor to a set of double doors. He lightly leans against the bar on one of the doors, pushing it open as quietly as possible. His brown face peers into the poorly lit room.

Gloom pulses through the room, with only small dots of light poking out from curious holes in the ceiling. Caleb urges open the door some more — the room is empty, or so it looks. The curious teen pulls his phone out of his pocket, using the light from the screen to guide them further into the room's depressing darkness. Once they're just a few steps in, they hear faint voices off in the distance.

"They're in here," Caleb whispers to the others.

"We know that, Cal, but what are they doing in here?" Jaylen says.

"The same reason we are in here… Hiding." Faint cries of despair from outside the solid structure tickle at their eardrums. "You hear that? It's a war out there." Caleb's blunt statement frightens Micky, the thought of an early death pounding around in her head. She latches onto Caleb's arm like a girlfriend tiptoeing through a haunted house.

The teens reach the foyer and immediately get startled by the unmistakable sound of glass shards crunching and crackling beneath their feet. They do their best to mute the sharp noises, slowing their pace but still pressing on. The women are just up ahead, now using lanterns to guide them as they enter the darkest part of the long-forgotten mall.

"We can't lose them," Caleb starts. "Let's see where they are going." The teens exchange a look of unease with one another, their eye contact a note of assertion to keep moving forward. They take a step forward, and out of nowhere a small group of people races by. The teens jump back, hesitating their next move. Caleb shrugs his shoulders and follows after the newcomers with Micky, while Jaylen lags behind, keeping a comfortable distance just in case the need to make a run for it presents itself.

Ahead, the small cluster of runners pivots on their heels, turning into a large showroom. A beloved town staple, Joyce's Department Store, occupied this particular space once upon a time. Outdated machinery and moth-eaten furniture take up the entire space of the old store lobby. The center aisles that once were now remain as nothing more than a row of decaying pillars. Stacks of dusty wood line the store's perimeter. With ceilings extending thirty feet high, along with a massive skylight covering a good portion of the room, disrepair has made it nearly impossible to see the outside world beyond. Pile after pile of debris climb to the ceiling, suffocating the area around the skylight itself.

Toward the front of the room, an assembly of citizens gather, their eyes glued to a single man heading the meeting. Those in the first row have tiki torches to help light the space. The man up at the front is not messing around. He has rose-colored cheeks, a head of wavy brown hair, and a police badge dangling around his neck. Appearing strong in character, the officer's accent proves itself to be just as strong – and fresh off the Jersey Shore.

"We have a choice to make," the officer says, the only commanding presence in the room. "We sit on our hands, waiting for death, or we take death to their doorsteps." He paces, revving up the crowd with his hate speech, aggression quickly building. The feisty group hoots and hollers, some pumping their fists in agreement with the man's deplorable notion. Assorted white faces peer out from the crowd, glowing under the tiki torches with absurd delight at the words being spewed. The bystanders stare up at the man with adoration as if it's the Second Coming of Christ, throwing various coins and dollar bills at his feet. Several of the attendees have guns strapped to their sides. The officer encourages the crowd to settle down, his voice resuming to a moderate level as he continues, for fear of being heard by the Akache.

"We got to stand strong and rid our country of these roaches. They will surely bring disease and famine to our shores. We've got to act now! Every one of the Blacks are joining forces with these invaders. Where does that leave our kind? Before long, there will be no more naturally blooded Americans left to preserve our freedoms." The rebels pump themselves up, hoisting their tiki torches high into the air with defiance, effortlessly throwing around hateful racist vulgarities like rice at a wedding.

Caleb, Jaylen, and Micky look on awkwardly, watching the rage-filled meeting in disgust. They hide from behind a pillar toward the back of the room.

"Cal, I don't think this is our kind of crowd," Jaylen whispers.

"Who you telling?"

The angry mob stands at the front of the room, torches still lifted, chants filling the air in the distance. "Give me freedom, or give me death!"

"Oh, they'll have death real soon," Jaylen says assuredly with a grin.

"Stopping every Black from joining, even if it means death to them, must be our business," the officer at the head of the group announces.

"What?! This dude is racist, bro," Jaylen says, shaking his head in disgust.

"They are as serious as a heart attack," Micky says, breaking her silence. "It's frustrating since we have come so far."

"Far?!" Caleb turns to Micky. "I hear that rhetoric on every cable news channel. I wouldn't necessarily give America an A+ on progressing from racism."

"Welcome to the party, Caleb," Jaylen says. "Finally, you are realizing what I've been saying."

"Jaylen, I've never said there wasn't pockets of racism across the country. I just choose to see the good in people."

"Yes, and the 'good' people will stab you in the back and ask you to clean the blood from the floor. That's America."

Micky gets right into Jaylen's face. They stand toe to toe. "Not true," Micky spews. "Everybody is different, Jaylen. You can't paint everyone with a broad stroke."

"Sure, you can, it's happened to us for four hundred years."

"But you weren't even here four hundred years ago."

"So what?! My people were," Jaylen continues, his voice rising with anger.

"You are not making sense, Jaylen," Micky says, matching Jaylen's tone.

"Not to mention they killed Michael, Whitney, and Prince too. Show me the lie, Micky!" Jaylen says, huffing. The rowdy spectators at the front of the room overhear the commotion, ceasing their impromptu assembly. Each person in the group turns toward the disagreeing teens cowering in the dark.

"Who's out there?!" the main leader roars. Caleb, Jaylen, and Micky squeeze themselves even further behind the fallen pillar, fearing for their lives. "Come out… Or else we will shoot you out." One by one, the frightened teens emerge from their hiding place, stepping into the light of the torches. "What the hell y'all doing in here?"

"They're spies," a woman with a major gap in her two front teeth shouts from amid the crowd. The leader steps down from his makeshift soapbox, a crate he was using to stand high above his followers. Parting the crowd, he now stands within a few feet of the nervous teens. He targets Micky first, glaring into her eyes.

"Why are you with them?" he asks.

"They are my friends," Micky answers.

"Traitor to your own people? You should be ashamed."

"And you're a cop," Micky says. She shoves her way in between Caleb and Jaylen, using herself to shield them, her eyes fixed on the badge dangling from the man's neck. "It's your duty to protect and serve, no matter the circumstances. You should be ashamed; not I."

"Do you see what's going on out there? It's war, and they are winning. We have to stick together, or else we suffer extinction."

Micky shrugs off his arrogant comment with a roll of the eye. "Delusions of grandeur at its finest!"

"Look here, little lady," the officer warns, "don't get smart with me."

"I'm not afraid of you!" Micky says, looking as though she's preparing to lunge. Caleb holds her back. "It's people like you who give white people a bad name."

Jaylen suddenly takes a cautioned step forward. His eyes first lock onto the man's golden badge. Next, he studies his face. The teen's body tenses up, shaking with trepidation. Hot tears trail down his cheeks in silence as his blood boils from within. This is the most control Jaylen's displayed since the takeover began. But his friends don't even notice the silent tears, the boiling blood – until it's too late…

Through the modest crowd, Jaylen sneaks around undetected, snatching a shotgun out of the hand of a crazed woman. He aims the gun at the man with the badge.

"It's you," Jaylen whispers with intensity. "I remember that face. Five foot ten. Brown hair. A skull tat on your left forearm, and a mole under your right sleepy ass eye. I'll never forget your face. Herald Turner!"

"So, what's it to you, little fella?" the man says, slowly turning to face Jaylen.

"You killed my father." A mighty gasp echoes throughout the room. The vile man laughs off Jaylen's accusation, throwing his head back in amusement.

"You got to be kidding me, fucker."

"No, I'm not," Jaylen emphasizes by sending a round into the ceiling. Everyone immediately disperses, taking cover any place they can find, leaving their 'leader' alone in the line of fire. Jaylen rests the barrel of the gun on the man's chest.

"Jaylen, don't do this," Caleb pleads.

"Shut up, Cal, he killed my father! This punk bitch killed my father!" Jaylen looks to be on the edge of breaking down.

"Jaylen," Caleb says, walking over to Jaylen. "It's okay. I got you." He places a soothing hand on his friend's back.

"He's dead, Caleb. This fucking loser killed him!"

"Look, if I killed your father, I'm sure it was accidental," the man defends himself, lifting his hands in aggravated surrender.

"That weak ass apology isn't good enough. Get on your fucking knees!" From the other side of the room, the entire gathering of spectators watch in complete silence, some holding their breath without even realizing it. Caleb nonchalantly steps in front of Jaylen, ignoring the gun that's currently jammed in the man's chest.

"For a long time, I defended people like you," Caleb says in a beefed-up tone. "You breed hatred and shout it on every street corner to those who will listen," he says, motioning to the others scattered through the dimly lit room. "It's sad that we have to be on our knees in order for you all to appear taller. What are you without racism? Who would you actually be without your propaganda, lies, and deceit? Are you any good at anything? Do you even like yourself? Your kids? Again, I ask you – who are you without racism?"

Every single soul in the room takes a moment to reflect inwardly. Most look away, trying to compromise with the truth they've just heard. Caleb continues.

"We want the same thing you want for your families – to live peacefully among others without fear of retaliation and hatred. Officer, if my friend decided to blow off your fucking head, he wouldn't be wrong and he wouldn't be right. But I'm sure it would be accidental..."

For what seems like a moment of eternity, the room contemplates, soaking in Caleb's carefully constructed words.

"We didn't bring Akache here. So, pry your hands from your guns and bigotry. Help us find a way to survive together."

Caleb's next move is unforeseeable. Slowly, he glides his hand up the barrel of the gun that Jaylen holds. He gives it a gentle tug, lowering its aim to the ground. Without notice, a bang ricochets in the distance. Caleb's body boomerangs unexpectedly, colliding with one of the downed pillars, breaking it clean in half.

"You shot him!"

Chapter 14
Love Fight

The sun has started its peaceful descent, dipping ever so slightly below the horizon. Battles continue to rage on across America, with the Akache warriors already having conquered twenty of the fifty states. The United States military has fought long and hard over the past day, struggling to hold off the mysterious alien invaders — but they are nowhere near close to defeating their more powerful combatants.

From deep inside the abandoned Genesee Mall, amid the ramshackle survivor's camp, comes the faint sound of a woman weeping. A decrepit old store serves as the backdrop of a devastating mishap. Several weak lanterns flicker on and off, casting eerie shadows and a feeling of uncertainty over the room and its current occupants.

Micky kneels over Caleb's lifeless body positioned awkwardly on the ground, her face buried in Jaylen's chest. Jaylen forces himself to be the strong one in the moment, fighting back tears like a world-weary pro.

Spectators gradually crowd around Caleb, each one struggling to push down inner turmoil as regret from their own earlier behavior rises to the surface. Caleb lies facedown on the cold, hard concrete, a river of his blood drawing a line from his gunshot wound to Herald's shoes. The officer notices the blood but turns away. He approaches the assailant who pulled the trigger, a gentleman in his sixties with an atrocious combover, and snatches the gun from his hands.

"Herald, I thought that son of a bitch was going to shoot you," the man says, pleading his case.

"Well, you made a mistake, Mr. Lawson – and now, he's dead."

"I had no way of knowing if he was going to shoot."

"Go to hell, you racist bastard," Jaylen says, angrily leaping to his feet. "Let me guess… You were afraid. How come y'all always afraid with a weapon in your hand? Come up with another script, you deadbeat!"

Jaylen shakes his head in inescapable disappointment, trying to momentarily mask the anger that rages within. A long moment of silence passes. All of a sudden, Jaylen launches himself at the unapologetic older man, using his chest to bully him into a tight corner.

"Why would you shoot? Why? He's gone because of you!" Jaylen looks back, staring at Caleb's lifeless body, still unable to believe he's really gone. The traumatizing moment of the murderous bullet racing for Caleb's innocent teenage body plays in a constant loop in Jaylen's mind, keeping his rage hyped to the extreme. His eyes follow the blood trail as it trickles out from Caleb's body. He comes to a heartbreaking realization… The chance to grow old with his best friend was stolen – stolen right out from under him by this puny, cowardly man.

Lifting his shoulders with care, the sorrow in Jaylen's face suddenly blanches. A deep inhale flows through his nostrils. Finally, the devastated teen turns to face the older gentleman, cocks back his fist, and slugs him hard, right on the chin.

"Chin-check, punk," Jaylen shouts, and with that, he's thrown down the gauntlet. A contentious game of tug-of-war breaks out, and it's Jaylen versus the defiant group surrounding him. Herald unexpectedly yanks Jaylen to safety, shoving him up against a pillar.

"Now, everybody, calm down," Herald begins. "Mr. Lawson, stay over there, and you, stay here." Herald uses force to drag Jaylen toward the entrance.

"No, screw this," Jaylen says, putting up a fight under Herald's grip. "I'm going to whack his old ass! He's white trash!" He struggles to free himself, swinging, throwing punches but to no avail. Herald breaks out his strength in full-force, wrapping his arms tightly around Jaylen's body like a python sucking the life out of its prey.

"I need you to calm down," Herald commands.

"Screw you, bro! The White Savior bit ain't working this time around. Shooting a man when he is down… That's right up your alley, right?"

"Look here, fella. I know we got off to a raw start, but you have to stay levelheaded."

"He's the one who shot my friend, and I have to calm down?! Miss me with that, Herald!"

"Well, are you going to let your friend die in vain?"

"Hell no, Mr. Lawson's going to get what's coming to him." Jaylen musters the strength to bash Herald in the shins. The officer immediately drops, clutching the fronts of his legs. The teen seizes this opportunity.

"You wanna kill him? Go right ahead and kill him!" Herald says, limping away. Instantly, Jaylen scoops up the murder weapon from the floor, cocks it, and aims it straight at Mr. Lawson's head. The old man panics and grabs a woman, utilizing her body as a shield.

"You fucking coward!" The edge of the barrel settles on the woman's shoulder, pushing her to one side. "Get out of the way," Jaylen shouts, tormenting the old man with his own gun.

Mr. Lawson shifts his weight onto his good leg, using his cane to keep his balance. The wrinkles worn into his aged face tell the tale of someone who's lived a long, hard life. He cowers back further into the corner.

"Don't shoot, please," Mr. Lawson starts. "I didn't mean it."

"You want mercy but are unwilling to bestow mercy onto others? Ain't that some white privilege shit!" Jaylen shifts the gun's aim from the old man's head, to his chest, pressing it in deeper, pushing his frail body to its limit. The bystanders watch intensely, some silently pleading for the old man's salvation, others pleading for their own.

"Please. Don't kill me." Mr. Lawson takes a sharp inhale as the tip of the shotgun glides from his chest and back to the center of his forehead.

"The funny thing is... You're already dead inside, and you don't even know it." The barrel of the gun trembles uncontrollably, Jaylen's shaky hands clutching onto it desperately. Emotions, unavoidable in this moment, consume him from the inside out.

He begins to think what advice his grandmother might provide at such a peculiar time as this. The nervous teen examines his unsteady hands, only one last question probing his troubled mind. Why shouldn't I smoke this a-hole? Managing to reconcile with his anger, Jaylen lets the gun slide from the man's forehead, to his chest — and to the ground.

"I can't do it," he murmurs, his hushed tone painted with disappointment. The loss of his best friend consumes him all at once with the weight of a Mack truck. He nearly drowns in the sudden wave of pain, the unbearable hurt igniting a feeling of wrath.

"Fuck!" Jaylen strikes the wall with a closed fist, an avalanche of tears flowing down his silky chocolate skin. "I hate this world. I swear, I do."

Jaylen's eyes glaze over the disturbing positioning of his friend's fallen body, permanently committing the horrific image to memory. Then all of a sudden, the muzzle of a nine millimeter kisses the back of the teen's head, the cold steel pressed hard against his skull. But Jaylen doesn't even care. He quickly makes peace with his maker and wishes to leave this awful world behind. Closing his eyes, he accepts the inevitable fate brought upon him by none other than Old Man

Lawson.

Before he can pull the trigger, Herald empties a bullet into the decrepit elder's chest cavity. The force slams Mr. Lawson's body into the wall, his fragile shape slumping to the floor. The injured old man peers up at Herald with a questioning look in his eyes. Glancing around the room for the slightest speck of praise or recognition but getting none, Herald looks quite pleased by his own actions. He sets his gun back into its holster and retreats to the shadows. A battered Jaylen wishes a silent thank you to Herald from across the room, nevertheless keeping a close watch on him. A hush falls over the room as everyone goes to their respective corners, meditating on the events that have just taken place.

Micky sits curled up in a ball on the floor, her lips moving in a silent prayer for Caleb's soul. She bows her head, concealing her tears from the strangers surrounding her. The teenager's untimely death seems to have taken its toll on everyone in the room.

An unexpected cough nearby severs the heavy silence. Micky and Jaylen instantly turn their heads. They notice Caleb's body weakly shifting on the floor.

"Cal! Cal!" Jaylen races to Caleb's side, screaming, unable to control himself. "He's not dead. He's not dead." Micky joins him.

Mystified, they watch as the pool of blood that was pouring from Caleb's veins just moments before now snakes its way back into his body. The incision within Caleb's chest ejects the bullet from the recent gunshot wound. Crouching down, Micky picks up the slug.

"That's eerie! How did he do that?!" Micky says, drawing the slug to her face, cupping it in her hands. "Don't move him, Jaylen. Caleb, can you hear us?"

"Look," Jaylen says, pointing at Caleb's body as it levitates, hovering just a few inches above the floor. All of a sudden, a warped white light shoots from his eyes and mouth. Engulfing all corners of the room, the distorted light forces everyone present to shield their eyes. The brilliant current permeates every inch of the sizable room for not longer than an instant — and then, as quickly as it came, the intense glow completely dissolves back into the atmosphere. The spectators around the room slowly come out from hiding, uncovering their eyes. Micky and Jaylen exchange a look and an almost simultaneous sigh of relief. As soon as her eyes readjust, Micky catches a glimpse of the intricate patterns lining Caleb's back. She pushes his shirt just so to reveal more of the curious designs.

"Whoa, look…" Micky says, gently tracing the markings with the soft pads of her fingers. "It looks like a map of sorts."

"A map? No, it looks like the crop circles in the fields," Jaylen counters. Micky reaches out to Caleb, placing a comforting hand on his neck, checking for a pulse.

"He's alive," she confirms. Caleb's body settles, gliding easily back to the floor. Wasting no time, Jaylen flips over his friend's body.

"Caleb!"

"Look, one of his eyes is gray. And what are those markings on his face?" Minuscule designs of the unknown are now etched into the flesh of Caleb's face. A few long moments pass as his friends try to make sense of the new markings. Finally, Caleb sits up, unconcerned as if this whole coming back to life thing was an everyday occurrence, no big deal.

"How long was I out?" the teen casually asks. Every soul in the room gasps at once, shocked and confused. Micky and Jaylen immediately cozy up beside Caleb, showering him with hugs.

"Yo, don't do that again, bro," Jaylen says, his voice tight with emotion.

"What are you saying, Jay?"

"I'm saying that a-hole tried to take you

out." The sound of a piercing wail suddenly overtakes the room, emanating from the heavens high above.

"Shhh, you hear that?" Micky says, cautiously rising to her feet, worried eyes desperately searching in all directions. The entire group of spectators gradually meet at the center of the room, their attention captured by the lightly cracked skylight overhead. From amid the shadows comes an alarming whisper.

"They have found us." The noises seem to grow louder and louder, closing in on them more urgently with each passing second. Regardless of whose side they're on, each and every person in that room backs themselves into a circle, bracing for the beastly presence that seems to be heading their way. Those with guns raise their weapons skyward, waiting, dreading… Then it happens – the glass skylight shatters, releasing countless shards over the citizens below. With that, everyone scatters like mice struggling to escape an abandoned ship. They are nowhere near ready for what is yet to come.

A small fleet of Akache warriors catapult through the skylight and into the mall. The terrorizing invaders take their place in front of the only exit, the only visible chance to escaping this nightmare. Rising in impressive synchrony, the warriors point their indestructible spears threateningly toward their panic-stricken opponents. The elongated athletic bodies of the triumphant warriors sway with purpose in an unsettling pattern of movement. Their faces, emotionless, are hidden by the shadows within the dark interior. Indiscernible writing covers the length of their arms and legs, the designs just faintly reminiscent of those etched into Caleb's back. The warriors settle their spears to the side of their bodies, pounding them on the floor in a particular succession of beats, an oddly harmonious sequence. The rhythmic thumping welcomes the descent of an additional body as it lands with power on one knee. For a better look, Caleb and Jaylen push their way closer to the front, eyeing the Akache warrior – it's a woman.

The Akache woman lifts to her feet with grace, towering over the two boys. The mahogany tint of her skin glistens in the morsel of light being offered from above. A sleek red-colored ponytail sprouts from the woman's otherwise bald head, wrapping itself around her neck and cascading down her shoulders. Her gray eyes are unique from the Akache men in that they give off a radiant beauty and mystery, rather than a look of pure hatred and destruction. The woman's body is that of an Amazonian goddess, muscles bulging from every part of her physique. A breastplate shields her chest. Bronze cuffs encircle her powerful biceps. Also unique from the Akache men is the deep indentation within her forehead — it's more pronounced, more awkward than the others. The female Akache warrior lifts her spear and shifts herself into an emotionless, unnerving fight stance. The thin stream of light from above shines on her with perfection.

Eyes locked on the striking female, Caleb's mouth drops, and in one smooth move he stands directly in front of her towering form. He tries to speak but nothing manages its way out. With her snout, the Akache woman sniffs the encompassing area, taking in a deep inhale of the boyish scent.

"Kahleo?" the woman asks in a foreign tongue.

"No, it's me, Caleb," Caleb says, taking another step forward. "Bree?"

"Bree??" Jaylen shoots a glance at Caleb, then cautiously approaches.

"Look, the tiny pink butterfly on her right shoulder. I can see her beyond the muscular exterior and the alien coat they have her wrapped in. That's Bree, Jaylen. She's alive." Caleb eases into it, taking his time.

Carefully he saunters over to the female warrior, inching closer and closer. This Bree personification before him is several inches taller, her sweet girlish figure having been replaced by a more powerful, more dominant one. Caleb tilts back his head, taking in the Akache warrior's savage-like features that have replaced those of the innocent girl he fawned over constantly through his teen years. Somehow, he senses her staring back at him. His eyes shift upward and he watches as she sways back and forth, trying to gauge the white light that radiates directly in front of her. Seizing the moment, Caleb reaches up, and using the back of his hand, caresses her face. Without a hint of warning, she knocks the curious teen onto his bum, flinging him thirty feet across the room. Damn, it's like that, Bree.

Rapid gunfire blazes from the direction of the frightened spectators. The bullets manage to strike Bree in the chest. They penetrate her flesh, entering her throat cavity, exiting out the back of her neck. Unharmed, the warrior releases a mighty growl and launches herself fifty feet into the air, using her spear to skewer the shooter's heart. The rest of the Akache warriors follow with an overwhelming, thunderous chant, commencing the start of an intense battle.

Bree springs from one side of the room to the other, declaring Micky as her first target. Micky does her best to wriggle free, but Bree grabs hold of her by the neck, squeezing every bit of life out of her.

"No, Bree! Stop it," Caleb shouts. Gasping for air, Micky struggles within Bree's death grip, her skin quickly turning a sickly shade of gray. She's losing oxygen fast — too fast. Caleb continues his plea. "You are going to kill her. Please, Bree, let her go!" Micky's flailing legs slowly settle down as her mind drifts off to a peaceful unconsciousness. The teens need to act fast, so Jaylen grabs a shotgun from the floor and uses it to smash Bree in the back. Roaring with a vengeance at the petrified teen, Bree turns, using her unbelievable strength to slap away Jaylen like a gnat. Then the victorious warrior hoists Micky high above her head, taking horrifying delight in the girl's early demise. Bree's hands are still gripped tightly around her victim's neck, squeezing tighter and tighter, until suddenly — Micky releases a dreadful scream.

Chapter 15
The Red Light

Mayhem runs wild throughout the twists and turns of the abandoned Genesee mall. Citizens make desperate attempts to overcome the Akache warriors but every last one fails. The forcible power of these unearthly beings reaches an apex as they trounce everything and everyone in their path effortlessly.

Suddenly an unnerving squeal echoes through one of the vacant hallways. Bree has Micky restrained at the neck, constricting her airflow. Micky's legs dangle helplessly. She's unable to save herself, and she knows it. The teen's body settles into stillness. Her eyes flicker, then drift shut as she inhales for what could be the last time.

"Bree, stop it!" Caleb shouts, frantically waving his hands to shift her focus. He runs to Micky's aid, planting himself directly in front of the monstrous creature. Bree's grip tightens. Her eyes shine with pleasure. "Bree, it's me, Caleb. Please let her go."

Bree turns, suddenly fixated on Caleb. A soft moonlit glow outlines the shape of his body. Micky uses the distraction to pry herself free from Bree's eased grip. Her body flops loose, thudding hard against the ceramic floor. She uses the last of her strength to awkwardly stumble away, leaving Caleb behind.

Bree disregards Micky's escape, growing more mesmerized by the glow that parades softly around Caleb's form. The brilliant glow illuminates brighter and brighter. Bree sways, seeming to enjoy the light show that envelops Caleb's smooth mocha-colored skin.

"Bree, I know it's you. Can you hear me?" Caleb asks calmly as he takes a step closer. Bree pushes her foot forward, keeping a comfortable distance between them. Despite the raging Akache war that swirls around him, Caleb locks in on Bree, the only girl he's ever loved. "I see you, Bree. Please speak to me."

An unfamiliar growl emerges from Bree. She now clutches her spear tightly, urging even more distance between her and Caleb. When she sees Caleb is unafraid, she reaches out and uses her spear to gingerly poke him in the chest. Something's stopping her from annihilating the inquisitive boy.

Frustrated, Caleb staggers back just enough to keep her anger at bay. "Come on, Bree. I know you're in there. Fight. I need you to fight."

The spear settles at Bree's side. A slight wave of ease comes over her face. The surrounding Akache soldiers line up, forming a barrier around the two teens.

"Please, Bree, come back to me," Caleb pleads.

Suddenly the Bree who Caleb has known his entire life seems to emerge. In her distinct American accent, she struggles to choke out words. "Caleb, please help me. It won't let me go."

"I'm going to help you, Bree. Stay calm. We can reverse this thing."

A piercing snarl of despair spews out Bree's mouth as she fights to remain present. Her strength weakens and her fear becomes apparent. "It won't let me out, Caleb. I want to go home."

Just then, Jaylen leaps over a mound of massacred bodies and sprints to Caleb's side. "Oh my God… It is her! How do we get her out?"

"I don't know, Jaylen."

Herald watches from the shadows as one by one his counterparts lose the battle and their lives. He waits for the right moment to strike. He steps out into the light, fists clenched and jaw tightened as if gathering the strength to jump from a plane. Without warning, Herald points his gun and fires a barrage of bullets straight into Bree's back. The slugs almost immediately exit her chest before exploding into countless pieces.

"NO!!!" Caleb screams. Bree's sinister warrior persona makes a return, with growls bigger, louder, and more vicious than ever. Her fangs protrude with rage, frightening any remaining onlookers. The female warrior's already muscular frame somehow expands even further right in front of their eyes. Pivoting swiftly, Bree stalks Herald like a panther in the wilderness, backing him into a corner. She lifts her spear high above her head, ready to bring it down onto his head with full-force. Her fierce snarl, a reminder of the unbeatable battle ahead, echoes through the space.

"She's going to kill him," Jaylen yells sharply. Hoping to repay the officer for his recent heroics, Jaylen makes a valid attempt, trying to shield Herald from the danger that is bound to come. Bree keeps her demented eyes locked on her prey, while lifting her palm ever so slightly. The movement effortlessly lifts Jaylen from the floor. With a forceful punch of her hand, air meeting air, she sends the teen skidding uncontrollably into the shadows.

"I can't feel my legs, Cal," Jaylen screams from across the room. "I can't move!"

Herald shifts his head toward Jaylen. A subtle smile appears on his face as he accepts the unavoidable fate that awaits him. He follows with a regretful apology not a moment too soon.

"I am sorry about your father," Herald utters. At that moment, the barbarous weapon plunges deep into Herald's heart. He falls to his knees and collapses on the uncomfortable floor, perishing instantly like all the others. By now, bodies are stacked like sardines in the rundown space, every inch of the dimly lit battlefield reeking of death.

Caleb and Jaylen take cover behind a pillar, joined by two other surviving African Americans. Micky is left to fend for herself. With every ounce of remaining strength left within her body, she struggles, fighting hard to stay alive. She digs her fingernails into the wooden boards, giving it her all — but it's futile. She's simply too weak.

Unable to sit idly by as his friend withers away, Caleb rushes out from behind the pillar of safety. He throws his body atop hers, shielding her as best he can. The other two African Americans follow his lead. Still unable to move properly, not having regained feeling in his legs yet, Jaylen lags behind. Bree snarls with rage as she watches the others come to Micky's aid. She signals the Akache warriors. Instantly, they respond, pointing their spears at the pile of dead bodies.

"Acha ca mula," Bree chants, staring ahead with a stern glare.

"What is she saying?" Jaylen whispers to Caleb.

"She says that we are traitors to the Belivian race here on Earth," Caleb says in a whisper barely loud enough for the others to hear. The Akache warriors, including Bree, hoist their spears skyward, their oversized feet lifting several inches off the floor. They begin rising higher and higher skyward, stopping fifty feet in the air. The fleet ominously circles the helpless citizens below, hovering ceremoniously, with evil at the center of their fight.

From her place in the sky, Bree glares down at the pile of bodies on top of Micky, refusing to budge. The brazen warrior summons a conniving chuckle that sends shivers up and down spines. With that, the entire Akache fleet plunges back inside the dilapidated mall with unimaginable force, ready to finalize their win. Any and all surviving patrons take cover wherever they can manage, scattering throughout the large room in terror.

"Brace yourselves!" Caleb screams to the others, covering his head, his body still thrown over Micky's frail form. The fleet's descent builds in speed and momentum, amping up their power to the fullest extent. Landing with their signature move, they take to the ground on both knees. Red light flares shoot out from their bodies, mysteriously emerging only to connect with the floor, creating a blazing red funnel leading to the opening in the shattered ceiling above.

Slowly, the funnel lifts Caleb and the others several feet into the air, leaving Micky's barely conscious body out in the open, ready for attack. As the others float weightlessly into the rose-colored light calling them forward, the ear-splitting blare from Lanier University makes an unwelcome return. Everyone except for Micky and the warriors clamps their hands to their ears in pain.

Micky's body remains on the ground below, unable to move no matter how hard she tries. Bree rises to her feet, enjoying the show, ready to put an end to it once and for all. Caleb glares down helplessly, floating high above, enveloped by the red haze. All of a sudden, the Akache warriors lifts their spears in succession and launch themselves into the air again, with only one target on their mind. Primal fight-or-flight takes over from deep within Micky's soul, and with a fast-fading burst of energy, she manages to hoist herself to her feet. She looks around and finds herself encircled by an array of weapons that keep coming closer and closer. Her heartbeats thump across her ribcage, tears streaming down her face uncontrollably. She makes peace with her horrifying demise, like the others before her. Her eyes close as the threatening spears around her inch forward. The teen stands amid the red haze, praying her final prayer.

"I'm sorry. I should have done more," Micky whispers to no one. Everyone else is high in the air funnel, safely hovering within the brim of the clangorous red glare. But perhaps all hope is not lost — Caleb summons strength from the very core of his being. His body swings upright and suddenly he floats through the air with controlled movements, watching with intensity as the spears below close in on Micky's chest. He refuses to give up without a fight. Caleb opens his arms wide, evoking a blinding light that shoots from the center of his body, followed by his eyes and mouth. The white light overtakes the entire space, rippling down from the top of the room, to the floor. Once making its way to the Akache fleet, it commands an extreme dominance over the warriors. The powerful light propels forward like an unstoppable force, tearing through the room with uncontainable fury, driving each warrior upward and out through the skylight. Finally, everything settles; the light recedes and the normal state of Caleb's body returns. He floats downward in silence, his strength officially exhausted, his fragile form landing in the center of the room in a fetal position, unmoving. The others spiral uncontrollably toward the ground, the pile of dead bodies breaking their fall with ease.

Jaylen's the first to get to his feet, still with only partial feeling in his lower extremities. He limps over to his friend. "Caleb. Caleb, bro. Can you hear me?"

Caleb groans. "Yeah, I can hear you." He slowly moves to a seated position, pulling himself up.

"Bro, what in the bloody hell was that? You were like a bomb or a weapon, clearing this bitch."

"I don't know. It was like I was directed to do it from some force."

"Cal, I need that force… There are a couple of knuckleheads I'd love to use that on."

"Aside from that mountain of bodies over there, I'm okay," Caleb replies ignoring Jaylen's remark. He stands, uneasy on his feet, wobbling from side to side. Jaylen helps him regain his footing, throwing an arm over his friend's neck. The two examine the perimeter, catching sight of Herald's lifeless body lying facedown under a stack of wooden planks.

"Is Micky okay?" Caleb asks. The other two surviving African Americans stand over the teen girl's lifeless body, sadness showing in their eyes.

"I think she's dead."

Chapter 16
I Cannot Tell a Lie

By now, nearly every window and door has been boarded up across the globe. Families of all colors, races, and creeds have gone into hiding. Most sequester themselves in basements, the hope of being reunited with society only a distant dream. Households everywhere sit waiting on pins and needles for the President's official address to the nation. Those walking the streets are limited to a few brave African Americans. Some offer help to their white neighbors out of the goodness of their heart, providing food, aid, and medicine. Rival gang members hold bidding wars among white families, presenting them with the service of protection against the Akache in the surrounding urban neighborhoods. Akache flags have been planted on the property of almost every United States government building.

Saturating the atmosphere is a damning red mist, casting a thick fog, hard for the average American to see through. The perplexing mist infiltrates neighborhoods all around the world, oozing rapidly from the daunting Akache ships that hover overhead. Rumors fly surrounding the curious mist. Some say it enhances the Akache warriors' power, penetrating their robust shells and siphoning itself into their skin with ease. Scientist Mark Fitz has already taken it into his own hands, measuring data to either support or deny the speculation of the mist's purpose, but a solid conclusion has yet to be reached. Detroit and Chicago in particular have managed to become major hotspots for the evolution of the alien invaders. Lines extend for miles as thousands upon thousands of African Americans gleefully abdicate their citizenship, ready, willing, and waiting for their chance to join the infamous Akache army.

The towering warriors, with spears and shields hoisted high into the air, mobilize around predominantly urban cities, vehemently promoting the right to be Belivian. Running amok throughout the streets, the warriors recite a disturbing chant, their hypnotic murmurs willing all African Americans within earshot to commit their lives to the beastly Akache mission. Every now and then, a struggle breaks out between those willing to join the Akache — some resolve with a spirited debate, while other resolve with nothing short of death. African Americans who choose to stand with America, refusing to conform, find themselves always on the run from persecution. Black churches around the world hold revival services in hopes of educating others of their right to assemble with whom they deem as the enemy.

Suspended high in the sky, free for the world to see, is a prominent Akache crest. The vibrant colors featured on the crest wrap devilishly around the planet's weaponry. Spectators gawk with displeasure at the crest as it arches across the naked sky. Iowa and Oregon have quickly earned their reputation as the two states with the most resistance and highest death tolls. White Americans band together with the military, trying their hand at combatting the foreign invaders – but the fearsome strength and power of the Akache is overwhelming, trampling any obstacles in their path.

Meanwhile, at Camp David, President Reid braces himself for the first press conference since the invasion. Homeland Security Advisor Brad Doley waits in the next room over for his chance at getting in some presidential face-to-face. President Reid walks through a hallway, following after Molly, his Chief of Staff. She looks unsettled, her face painted in angst, her hair set atop her head in an unkempt bun. She hasn't slept in days and has the bags under her eyes to prove it. The

President marches his way down the short hall with the hidden mountain. He pauses, rubbing his fingers against his clammy palms, not quite ready to face the paparazzi. Taking a breath, he loosens the tie around his neck. Molly secures an American flag pin onto his suit jacket, symbolizing freedom for all.

"Thank you, Molly, for keeping it together," President Reid utters softly. Molly tries her best to hold back the emotion but silent tears soon manifest. "How's your family?" The fragile woman shakes her head, a look of sadness pouring from her eyes. "How bad is it?" Molly takes a small gasping breath to quell her tears for a moment.

"My mom's dead. And I can't reach my brother." The weary Chief of Staff inhales her tears, exhales with finality, and hands a briefing folder to the President. "So, you want to hit these points," Molly begins, her words comes fast and carelessly fused with anger. "Things are under control, we don't blame African Americans personally for their choices, and the galactic terrorists won't win."

"Molly," President Reid says, clasping both of Molly's hands in his own. "It's okay. We will get through this." The great man in power awkwardly embraces his Chief of Staff, but the professional she is, Molly won't allow herself to accept the warm gesture. She pulls away gently, nervously pushing back a few strands from her face.

"I'll be fine," she murmurs, mildly embarrassed. The President continues up the hall toward the moment of truth, his head now anxiously buried within his notes. His mind elsewhere, President Reid mistakenly trips over Doley's foot.

"Mr. President, did you feel it?" Doley sputters.

"What are you talking about, Doley?" President Reid asks, peeking up from his notes.

"The power of the white light – it was on every channel," Doley responds. The President stares back at him blankly. "It briefly stalled the battle, sending those motherfuckers back to their ships."

"Nuclear? Where did it come from? Russia? North Korea?"

"I doubt that, Mr. President. Both of them are already waiting with bated breath for the demise of our union."

"Is it a weapon?"

"We don't know, sir."

"Well, there's nothing more to talk about, then." With the advisor unable to provide the desired answers, President Reid continues making his way toward the press conference. Doley lingers, watching with an inquisitive eye as the most powerful man in the world walks away, entirely unbothered by the new information he has just received.

Ten journalists and a handful of select credentialed reporters cram inside the small press room, waiting patiently as President Reid enters. He stops at the podium, first glancing around at the few reporters, then staring down at the journalists seated before him. His nerves become more rattled with each passing second.

"Good evening," the President states. A somber welcome awaits him. He flips open his folder in preparation. His eyes catch a glimpse of a red light as it ignites on the camera set up at the back of the compact room. Suddenly paralyzed, his probing mind races and races, barely able to grasp onto what he should tell the American public. The surrounding journalists chomp at the bit, just waiting for the chance to crowbar in some questions of their own. President Reid anxiously rakes his fingers through his hair. He stares down at the prepared notes in his folder, then closes it up, choosing to speak from the heart. Clearing away a lump in his throat, he stares directly into the red light.

"My fellow Americans," President Reid begins. "I come before you on this tragic evening. I will keep this brief, and I will be honest with you. Bear with me. Sometimes honesty hurts, but I'll be prudent about the information I am about to disclose. In the last few days, our country has been attacked. Our brothers and sisters have been accosted and some killed. The entity who has chosen to go to war with us is called 'Akache.' We don't know much about them. Our intelligence team hasn't yet figured out the origins of these horrific beings. Information about these invaders are limited for a reason. We are asking all Americans to stay indoors. Barricade yourselves inside your homes. Run and hide as we work to get these acts of terrorism under control. I assure you — we have the best military on the planet. Our men and women are top-notch, and we will not be defeated! They are actively working, fighting hard to ensure our democratic freedoms continue. I can't lie. It won't be easy from this point on, but as God is my witness, we will get through this traumatic time."

Lights flash across the row of cameras at the back of the room, distracting the President, momentarily halting his near perfect speech. He inhales, getting himself back in the zone.

"For those Americans who have been inquiring, my family is safe in an undisclosed location. Unfortunately, the Akache has brought this fight to our doorstep only; our global family has chosen to stand down. Although as a nation we will fight this war alone, be assured our global family is rooting for our success. I look forward to the day when we will be reunited as a nation. God bless you, and God bless the United States of America." President Reid steps back from the podium ever so slightly as he releases his final words. Immediately, the reporters bombard him with an onslaught of questions.

"Hello, Mr. President, I am Cindy from Persons Magazine. How sure are you that we will defeat these monsters?"

"I am confident our military will do exactly what they are enlisted to do – protect and serve," the President answers in earnest. A slew of hands reach for the sky, flailing with objections. President Reid points to a female reporter in the corner. She steps forward.

"Mr. President, the last time Homeland provided us with information on the casualties, there were four hundred thousand white Americans killed in battle, not counting those lives lost in the military. Is it fair that African Americans in the military are placed on the front lines, based on the enemy's preference to leave them unharmed?"

President Reid returns a blank stare to the woman, then turns to Molly, who hovers near the door. He's unsure of his response.

Molly steps up toward the podium, her voice carrying over the rowdy mob. "I'm sorry, but that's a false narrative. Although the Akache regime has coerced our African American brothers and sisters into participating in their devious plan of overtaking our country, we are certainly confident that our military generals know how to fend them off." She steps away, leaving President Reid to resume his post.

A harsh voice booms with vigor from the side of the room. "How do you reconcile in your mind that 70-percent of African Americans have chosen to side with a foreign adversary?" An intense hush falls over the room as everyone turns to the lone African American reporter asking the question. President Reid surely expected the tough questions to come amid such a situation – but not this soon.

"Well, I must say, we have a passionate and lovely African American community in our country. We haven't always gotten it right, but we have made strides to live up to what our Founding Fathers wanted for all men, regardless of creed, sex, religion, or race."

The others in the room stay quiet while the Black reporter continues his round of questioning. "There has been talk on the Hill that the United States has finally considered reparations, closing the wealth gap, and police reform. Why is the Hill taking up these policies now, when there is such an imminent threat encroaching on our country?"

"Thank you for the question," President Reid says, stalling. "We have never been placed in a unique situation like this. Those policies you are speaking of have always been on my agenda. Furthermore— " The reporter cuts off the President.

"I'm sorry, Mr. President, but both bodies of Congress have deemed those policies dead for the past three years. Again, I ask… Why now?" The soft ticking of each passing second rings out from the analog clock on the back wall, penetrating the silence in the loudest way possible, breaking President Reid's train of thought. As the President stares back awkwardly, every reporter in the room shoves forward their digital devices, trying to capture the inevitable impromptu response. But nevertheless, true to form, President Reid wavers not in his state of professionalism, choosing each word with care before speaking. He gazes up at the clock, frozen in place as he watches the second hand move at a snail-like pace. Finally, he again turns to his Chief of Staff.

"One final question, please," Molly screams over the restless group of reporters.

"After the Melanin Experiment debacle, how can you be assured that African Americans can trust the United States government again?" another reporter asks, their voice ringing out above the others.

"This country has been great for the Black community. Has it been perfect? No. Have we progressed? Yes."

"Then explain – why are Blacks enlisting in the Akache army at such an alarming rate, Mr. President?"

"I don't have the actual figures…" President Reid stammers. The reporter doesn't give up so easily.

"Your administration estimates that one in three Blacks are joining forces with the Akache."

"Again, I am unaware of the actual figures."

"Should they be ashamed of their allegiance to the Akache?" the reporter prods.

President Reid takes a deep breath, thinking long and hard before speaking. He places his folder under his arm, buying himself a few more seconds. The following words ring out crisply with poignant clarity. "They'd better hope they are on the right side of history." More questions rip through the space as the President gets swept away into another room.

Minutes later, President Reid paces alone in the Situation Room. The press conference replays over and over in his mind, wishing he could have better prepared for such an off-the-cuff performance. Molly bursts through the door.

"He's on line one," she says. "The television is connecting, Mr. President." She walks back out as quickly as she came.

President Reid forces himself to a halt. His intense stare lands on the phone sitting on the table across the room, watching the flashing red button. The President approaches the phone, removing his suit jacket and placing it on the back of his chair. He allows his index finger to graze over the button, muttering a silent prayer before pressing it.

"Fitz, talk to me."

"Are you alone?" Mark Fitz's voice asks over the other end of the line.

"Yes, I'm in a secure room."

"They have a weakness," Fitz begins, his words coming out shakily but assured.

"Go on, continue," the President prompts.

"The Navy SEALs cornered one of those bastards – and captured it."

President Reid's eyes widen as big as saucers. "Okay, tell me more."

"President Reid, they are terribly strong and powerful. That bastard killed forty SEALs before they took it down."

"Is it dead? Can we kill them?"

"No. We hit it with a tranquilizer, which lasted only sixty seconds before we restrained it. Turn on your television, Mr. President."

President Reid grabs a remote off the table and turns on the television. Sitting on the edge of the table, he stares, intrigued by what he's about to see.

On the screen, Fitz, the wacky scientist, leads a cameraman down a murky hall. "If you look closely, you'll see it. We are calling this one 'STA 1.'"

The camera pans into a glass enclosure filled with the signature red mist of the Akache. Hidden within the mist is the muscular flesh of an Akache warrior, only its arm and leg slightly visible. The enraged beast sways from side to side but keeps itself bound by the airy fog. On the screen, the image freezes. President Reid turns back toward the phone.

"Okay, Fitz, what else do you have?"

"The kid's blood is a partial remedy."

"Fitz, spare me the technicalities. Tell me."

"I've extracted the plasma from his blood. Conducted numerous tests and came up with a quick remedy — the Akache vaccine."

"Brilliant," the President replies.

"Not so fast, Mr. President. It only gives us a five-minute window in which their strength is temporarily stifled. After the five minutes are up, they become stronger. It buys us just enough time while we kill them."

"Are you crazy?! The optics on that would be heinous. Those are Americans up there— Fitz, I'll get back to you." President Reid ends the call abruptly. He ensures the door is bolted, then goes back to the table for the remote. Replaying the compelling video, he pauses the feed on a close-up of the intricate markings etched within the Akache warrior's skin.

The President approaches the television. Shoving his glasses onto his face, he peers closely at the stunning designs. "This cannot be."

Chapter 17
The Unreadable Map

The dust has finally begun to settle after the heartache that just a little while ago reared its beastly head across the dreary mall. On its descent over the horizon, the sun helps conceal pyramids of dead bodies spread out among the vacant building. A glowing illumination comes from Jaylen's direction as his phone drifts over Micky's weak body splayed out in the main lobby area. Caleb sits at her side, doing his best to nurse her afflictions. Suddenly, Micky's eyes pop open wide, startling the few surviving bystanders in the room. The badly wounded teen takes a single inhale and immediately clutches her side in supreme agony. She unleashes a hair-raising screech as if someone had shoved a knife deep into her heart right then and there. Caleb helps Micky to her feet, her strength waning fast.

"We got to get out of here," Caleb hisses in her ear. "I feel them... They will return. They will come for you."

"Where do we go?" Jaylen asks.

"I don't know, but not here." Caleb pulls Micky's arm around his neck and drags her along with him. Jaylen watches from the sidelines for a moment, and then reluctantly offers assistance to his friend. Now, both of Micky's arms wrap about the boys' neck as she drifts in and out of consciousness. Caleb leads the others toward a side window, crawling out to stumble into who knows what. Jaylen hesitantly nudges Micky's frail body through the opening. He makes it through last. Darting in between neighborhood houses, backyards, and more, they escape into the night.

As the three teens make their getaway to potential safety, they stop every now and then for Micky to catch her breath. Jaylen gives Caleb a look of uncertainty.

"Cal, she can't go any further. She won't make it."

"Okay… Let's try Perry Drugs," Caleb suggests as he spots the drugstore sitting on the street's West corner. The boys hurry over, dragging Micky to a stop at the side of the building. Jaylen rummages around for even a hint of an opening, but no luck — the store is as tight as they come.

"There's no way in," Jaylen concedes. "What do we do now?" Micky struggles to hold herself up but the pain becomes utterly unbearable. She slips down to her bum against the building, sitting through the worst of the insufferable pain surging through her entire body.

"She won't last out here. She needs medicine," Caleb says, kicking a rolling steel door with his size thirteens. The door doesn't budge in the slightest. Jaylen jumps up, snagging a limb from a nearby tree. He repeatedly whacks the wooden poker against the door's handle.

"There's got to be a way in," Jaylen says. The curious boy eyes a pile of random junk thrown into one corner and snags a crate. Standing atop the crate, he spots a minimal opening in the seal of the rolling door's window. He uses his elbow to break the glass, pushing it from the frame. Jaylen's slender body wriggles through the opening. On the outside of the rolling door, Caleb dabs at Micky's face in an attempt to keep her alert.

"Micky, you okay? Stay with us."

"I'm not going to make it," Micky croaks out. "I feel horrible."

"Sure, you are. Just keep talking," Caleb finishes, when all of a sudden, the rolling door pulls itself upward.

"Told you there's always a way," Jaylen says proudly, with a mouthful of chocolate. "All this running got a brother hungry." He helps Caleb usher Micky to the innards of the drugstore.

Inside, the store lies vacant, the glare of emergency lights bouncing through the store from back to front. The store has already been looted, merchandise scattered across nearly every square inch. Caleb sets his sights on an aisle, stopping to give Micky a chance to rest.

"Jaylen, stay with her. I'll be back."

"And why do I have to stay with her?"

"Because I said so," Caleb snaps. "I'll be right back." Caleb darts up the debris-filled aisle, leaping over toppled merchandise with nearly every step. Just before he reaches the other end, his sprint morphs into a crawl and finally a complete stop. He listens with intensity, his brown eyes widening as his gaze pans over the devastation caused by the looters.

Once deeming it safe enough to continue, Caleb leaps onto the pharmacy counter, refocusing his attention. The metal fence guarding the drugs has been snapped in half, leaving behind a tiny entry point. Wedging himself in between the sharp edges, Caleb races from counter to counter in search of the strongest pain medication he can get his hands on. His eyes scan labels. One by one, he shoves several bottles into his pockets. Once he's seen it all, he hops over the counter and races back up the aisle.

As soon as Caleb returns to Micky's side, he pops a pill into her mouth. Snagging an opened bottle of water from a nearby shelf, he forces the water down her throat. Jaylen tosses a neck pillow to Caleb from the front of the store.

"A neck pillow, Jaylen?"

"It's all they had," Jaylen answers, shrugging. Caleb smiles, gently positioning the pillow so as to cradle Micky's head.

"Thank you," Micky croaks out before turning over and drifting into a deep and comfortable sleep. The two boys leave Micky's side once they're sure she's asleep. They hop up onto a counter at the front of the store. The conversation is hesitant at first, each one waiting for the other to start. Jaylen begins, his voice in a quiet but comfortable tone, not loud enough for Micky to overhear.

"Caleb, you know they're going to find her."

"Yeah, I know."

"She'll only slow us down. I don't see this thing slowing anytime soon."

"So, what do we do, Jaylen? Just leave her here?"

"You said it; not me."

"But you were thinking it," Caleb counters.

"Let's try getting to my grandmother's house. It's like ten miles North of here."

"I'm not going to leave her to die, Jaylen."

"You left Bree – what makes Micky so different?"

"I resent that. I did not leave Bree. Micky needs us. It's the right thing to do. I would have thought you learned that by now."

"Okay, okay, I'll follow your lead," Jaylen assents. "But when those things come back—" Caleb jumps off the counter, pleading to his friend with an open stance.

"What are you going to do? Don't you get it? We have the upper hand. We have an opportunity to show them and the world that we are united." Jaylen rolls his eyes at Caleb's Kumbaya moment.

"I'm with you, Cal. But don't a part of you think this is God's will? His final judgment on an unjust race of people?"

"No. Man is flawed; not God," Caleb asserts. Jaylen leaps off the counter, his actions making it look like he's pleading his case in a courtroom. His head tilts curiously to the side.

"So, if man is flawed, kill their asses," Jaylen says with feeling. Caleb looks Jaylen up and down, shaking his head, wondering where the sweet, playful boy he's called 'friend' for the last decade has gone. Turning away to placate his feelings, Caleb shoves a fist forward, colliding with a bag of popcorn. Corn kernels shoot into his face wildly.

"That felt good," Caleb says, with doubt dripping from his affirmation.

"Caleb, your dreams that fateful summer day has brought us here. No one asked for this… Not even me. I'm just going with the flow of the river." Jaylen gets hit in the face by the store's blue emergency light, blinding him temporarily. He holds up a hand to shield his eyes from the blaring light. "Just like all the others, watching as our fellow brothers and sisters drown peacefully." The slightest morsel of guilt traces a path to Jaylen's heart. He hesitantly peers down the aisle at Micky's ailing body. "Okay, we'll take her ass with us."

"Let's grab the food that's left here, get some rest, and leave in the morning."

Several hours have passed by now. Caleb and Micky lie fast asleep on the ground. Jaylen nestles himself in a shopping cart, swiping through countless devastating images being posted on social media accounts from all across the globe. In the past hour, he's called his grandmother ten times — but no luck establishing communication as of yet. He's tried conserving his phone battery during this time as well, turning it off every now and then, usually for long stretches of time. In hopes of more pleasantly passing the time, the weary teen counts the number of ceiling tiles above him over and over.

Caleb lounges just inside the aisle's opening, a twelve-pack of toilet paper tucked underneath his head to help keep his neck at ease. His eyes twitch in the midst of his slumber. Random jitters take over the teen's body, racing up and down from his head to his feet. He suddenly yells out in his sleep, spewing words of gibberish. Seconds later, his body begins shaking violently, waking up Micky and Jaylen several yards away. Jaylen rushes over to the aisle, arriving just in time to get an eyeful of Caleb's contorting fit.

"Caleb, wake up," Jaylen says, rushing over to his friend. "You're having a bad dream." Caleb's body flops over onto his back, but something is wrong. His eyes protrude from out of their sockets, gazing around the dark room. The normal mocha tone of his skin has somehow transformed into a brown-reddish color, a hue similar to that of the Akache brood. Intricate markings etched into his face appear as big, bold, unreadable symbols, even more pronounced than usual. This new and improved Caleb stands at a whopping six foot six feet tall. His typical body form is scrawny, to say the least, but has suddenly transformed into that of a husky man – muscular, strong, and strapping. A golden shield is tied around his arm, including a bronze cape around his back to match.

Caleb's brand new dominant form explodes through the double doors, busting them right off their hinges. While roaming amid the scene, he sneaks a glimpse in his peripheral at a mob of angry white looters stomping around. Those in question are part of an anti-Akache group, each member of which dons heavy combat gear. They plant themselves in the middle of the street, protesting with their weapons shoved high into the air. Spacecrafts overhead send thunderous electrifying rays shooting downward, lighting up the red sky. Caleb releases himself, levitating just a few feet off the ground as more and more protesters gather around. They have forced themselves out of hiding with a single purpose in mind – taking on the fight of a lifetime with none other than the Akache. The bronze cape behind Caleb flails in the wind as he hovers about the ground. His hands suddenly shoot into the air, extending to the sky with pride.

He floats effortlessly, peering down at the boisterous group of protesters as they storm in his direction. Then it happens…

All of a sudden, thousands of sharp, spiraling tentacles extend from Caleb's raised hands, shooting up and embracing the red tinted nighttime sky surrounding them. Swirling razor-sharp blades jut out at the end of each tentacle. Down below, the protesters stare uneasily at the abundance of weapons at Caleb's immediate disposal. From his place within the sky, Caleb casts a menacing grin over the group, shifting his hands just enough as to send the pointed weapons nosediving their way onto the sea of people down below. Blood-curdling screams echo through the dim exterior as the threatening blades come crashing down, making contact with the heads of protesters, brain matter shooting every which way over and over until…

"Caleb! Wake up!" Finally, Caleb starts to awaken from the nightmare, his extremities flailing, kicking and punching. Jaylen shakes him vigorously. "Wake up!" Caleb's eyelids fly open in fear. He pushes away from his friend, looking around frantically, sweat beads forming along his upper lip.

"You had a bad dream, Caleb, but it's okay. We're here," Micky says while tending to a minor wound on her arm. Still jumpy and uncertain, Caleb scrambles to his feet, desperately shaking away the demented images left over from his nightmare.

"It was him; not me," Caleb starts. Jaylen keeps his distance, choosing not to make any sudden movements before finding out more.

"Who? Where?" Jaylen asks.

"Karnitu, the commander. He's trying to control me. He wants total control for his plan."

"Looks like he's succeeding. Those bodies are stacking up."

"I think," Caleb continues, lowering his voice as his eyes snake past Jaylen, "his plans are bigger than we thought. I sense that he's after something stronger, something more powerful." He begins pacing the front of the store, anxiety building with every passing moment. In a nearby mirror, he catches sight of his reflection, immediately spotting the additional writing now present on his arms. He takes in a sharp inhale, then frantically lifts his shirt from behind, doing his best to inspect the symbols along his back as well.

"Look at that. It's like the symbols are trying to tell us something," Caleb notes. Micky limps over. She glides her fingers down Caleb's back, her fingers tracing along the symbols, trying to piece together some semblance of information.

"I've studied the evolution of human history," Micky begins. "These symbols represent the existence of apelike creatures from millions of years ago. These creatures brushed our shores from Africa and migrated into Asia and Europe."

"So? And what does all that mean, Micky?" Jaylen spews in frustration.

"I'm not sure exactly. The designs here could be abstract, or may be giving a clue into the future… Maybe even a glimpse into our past—"

"These symbols are about our future," Caleb says, cutting off Micky's brainstorm. "The distinct designs represent the clashing of the past with the present." Jaylen curiously shakes his head, trying to make sense of the information his friends have just given. After a few moments…

"Okay, I'm lost," Jaylen confesses.

"Look at the points in which the symbols intersect," Micky says. "There are three poignant lines leading to this one symbol. That is the symbol of Diop. We can assume Asia, Africa, and Europe are these three points. They align with the fourth point. Why?"

“It’s the Book of Diop.” Caleb declares. “Old religion parables assure us that there were twelve disciples, but the rural study of theology translates these findings as false. There were actually only four disciples, each representing a point on the map on my back. Look at the lines, the monuments. It’s pretty clear.” Jaylen casts a skeptical eye toward the designs.

“That’s great and all, but how does knowing this help us?” Jaylen asks. Distracted, Caleb’s eyes open as wide as they can as he follows the symbols on his back from top to bottom.

“Oh, no,” Caleb mutters. Micky and Jaylen try waiting for the explanation that must inevitably follow, but their friend keeps it to himself for too long.

“What is it?!” Jaylen screeches impatiently.

“Now I know. Oh, my God, guys… How could we have been this stupid?!” Caleb lets out a deep exhale, trying to contain his erratic onslaught of emotions. “I know why Karnitu’s here.” Without any warning, a swarm of Secret Service agents burst through the double doors of the drugstore.

“Get your hands up!”

Chapter 18
The Reckoning

Pitch darkness has fallen over the gloomy nighttime sky. Three enormous tankers, each comparable in size to a Boeing 757, plod through a tunnel nestled between two colossal mountains. Armed guards patrol through the mammoth of the tanker. Caleb, Jaylen, and Micky have been sitting together for the past hour, waiting in nervous silence to see where their captors are taking them. The teens await their destiny in a cramped room, sitting around a square table. Jaylen's eyes are fixated on the single dangling lightbulb hanging overhead.

"This tanker gotta have cost a few million dollars, and they can't get a better light?" Jaylen snorts. "Fucking government… Always finding a way to waste our tax dollars." The tanker's bumpy ride through the mountains makes it hard for the teens to stay in their seats. Micky examines the curious writing along Caleb's arms, squinting as she tries to decipher the fresh scribblings. The medicine she ingested hours ago has since thrust her into a very happy place.

"You ever wonder where we go after we die?" Micky says, a glassy look in her eyes. "Because these hacks are going to kill us."

Silent tears begin to roll down her vanilla flesh. "All I wanted to do was help the Blacks."

"The Blacks?" Jaylen snaps, giving Micky a good dose of side-eye.

"Yes, Blacks, Negroes, African Americans," she insists adamantly. "I wanted to be an ally and fight the good fight. Fuck the police!" Micky catapults herself from the table, stumbling toward the locked door. "Yes, I said it," she shouts, pounding her fists against the metal door. "Fuck the police! Fuck the government! Fuck Akache! Free us now!"

"Cal, looks like the medicine has kicked in for your girl," Jaylen says, turning to Caleb.

"Yes, and I feel liberated, bitches," Micky babbles, her small frame playfully twirling around in a circle. "Why can't we all just get along? Wait, is the room spinning?"

"You're going to get us killed, white girl. Sit your ass down!" Jaylen huffs. "Caleb, how much of that stuff did you give her?"

"She was hurt pretty bad… I think 100 milligrams." Caleb and Jaylen watch as Micky suddenly returns to her seat, bringing her head down to meet the table.

"I feel sick," she groans. An unexpected knock bellows through the door.

"If we don't invite them in, will they still come in?" Jaylen asks, pouting with an attitude. The door swings open. In walks scientist Mark Fitz, his attention immediately caught by Micky's soon-to-be unconscious body. He takes her vitals, ensuring her livelihood.

"Hello, I am Mark, but you can call me 'Fitz,'" the slender, hollow-cheeked man says before turning his attention to Caleb. "I know who you are, Caleb." This brings about an enraged fist-pounding reaction from Caleb, who punches the table.

"Are we going through this again?!"

"I'll make this as brief as possible for you all."

"Now, you know y'all don't make nothing brief," Jaylen quips, leaning back in his chair, a coy look across his face.

"You see, Caleb," Fitz continues, ignoring the teen's snide remark. "You are exactly what this country needs."

"What are you talking about now?"

"You are going to single-handedly help bring Akache to its knees." The quirky scientist removes his glasses, wiping away any fog. Caleb sits up upon hearing this proclamation. He rolls his eyes but listens regardless of the absurdity.

"How are you planning to stop Akache?" the curious teen asks.

"With this." Fitz casually removes a bright red plastic gun from his pocket. Both Caleb and Jaylen tighten their grips on the table in front of them, keeping their mouths locked tight. "Inside this gun is a vaccine from your blood, Caleb. It controls them. You see, you are the science I've been seeking for a lifetime. Your DNA has such depth, regenerating cells right before our eyes. Your blood is a cure to this fight. Granted, one dose won't kill them, but within seconds, they'll be like you and me… Human."

"What happens when it wears off?" Fitz scratches his head at Caleb's question, probing deep within his mind for the perfect response.

"That's the part I'd rather show you. Get up." Fitz opens the door, leading the boys through the exit. Reluctantly, they follow him into the next corridor, immediately sandwiched between Fitz and five armed guards. Jaylen looks up at them, annoyed.

"Is this necessary?" Jaylen asks, both hands set on his hips. Fitz remains quiet for a few moments.

"Yes, very necessary," the scientist replies, without turning back. The roar from the tanker's engine makes it difficult to hear. Feeling ignored, Jaylen repeats himself, louder this time. He stops while turning up his lip.

"I said, is this necessary?" The tallest guard in the pack reaches out his meaty claw, grabbing hold of Jaylen and pushing him forward the moment he stops moving. Jaylen whirls around to size up the guard. "Hey, go easy, bro," the teen snaps. Thinking better of it, Jaylen willingly continues his trek as directed. The small cluster of people moving through the hall arrives at a metal door nearest to the rear of the tanker. The opening is heavily guarded by a squadron of military soldiers. Jaylen shifts himself closer to Caleb.

"Whoa, this tanker is huge! You could probably fit three houses in the place." Faint noises and scuffles come from behind the thick door, noises that are unfortunately familiar to the teens. They take a few measured steps back, accidentally entering the space of the soldiers immediately behind them. "Cal, I think they must have one of them inside there," Jaylen hisses.

Fitz waves aside the soldiers guarding the door. Red mist oozes out from the crevices of the door. Caleb and Jaylen clock the mist, sharing a look — they both know what waits on the other side. Fitz uses his keycard, slipping it inside the locking mechanism, to authenticate his access. The heavy door unlocks, slowly creeping open. Fitz leads Caleb and Jaylen through the door, the intense red mist enveloping the three of them as they make their entrance. He guides the boys in further, until they reach the spot where a reinforced steel cage sits. Waving away the mist, Jaylen is the first to approach the captured Akache creature standing before him.

"Stand back, boys," Fitz warns, stopping Jaylen in his tracks. They watch as the creature roams back and forth, concealed within the smothering red fog. It releases an unbelievably high-pitched screech, ferocious and intimidating. The teens curiously watch as Fitz steps closer to the cage, while they stay put. Fitz retrieves the red gun from his pocket. His beady blue eyes squint through the mist, searching for the predator. He aims the red gun in preparation.

"I think the mist protects them — you know, like crocodiles to water. I'm only doing this for their own good," Fitz tells the boys. The bass in Fitz's voice rattles the agitated creature, sending it spiraling into a beastly rage. It slams the entire weight of its body against the cage, vicious tremors shaking the massive tanker. Fitz doesn't panic in the slightest.

“There, there… Calm down. This will only take a few seconds,” he says, creeping closer still. The beast continues its destruction, pulling at the tungsten bars with otherworldly strength. Fitz refuses to back down, pointing and firing the vaccine missile into the cage. Immediately, the animal settles down and retreats into the confines of the red mist. Caleb intently watches the creature’s reaction, sauntering up to the edge of the cage. Fitz eyes Caleb curiously, fascinated by his display of bravery. The familiar Akache squeal emerging from the cage turns to a soft panting.

“Look!” Jaylen says, pointing at something protruding from within the haze – a human limb. A naked African American man appears from the mist, clutching tightly to the cage, eyes darting with fear. He’s weak. The last of his strength is exhausted as he tries to catch his breath.

“What happened?” the man asks breathlessly.

“If my calculations are correct,” Fitz turns to the boys, retrieving a stopwatch from his pocket, “we’ll have four minutes and thirty seconds.” He starts the timer.

“Please, let me out of here,” the caged man pleads. Fitz observes the man with care, keeping a close watch on the timer as the numbers rapidly decrease. Caleb and Jaylen watch the man, unsure of the proper response, but deep down rooting for his survival.

Only one minute passes before another transformation begins. The man's average-sized frame contorts violently, collapsing onto the hard metal floor of the cage. Curled up in a fetal position, he tries fighting off the jittery sensation but it effortlessly overtakes his human form. The bulging muscles make a reappearance. The half-human, half-beast concoction leaps to his feet, waiting for the moment in which his strength returns. Out of thin air, the chilling red fog rematerializes, encompassing its victim's body with a vengeance. The signature Akache ponytail sprouts from his head, extending the length of his naked body. But perhaps most shocking is what comes next — the hostile Akache warrior unleashes a spine-chilling howl, one that's never been heard before. Fitz's head snaps toward the door. He waves down one of the guards.

"Shoot it," Fitz calls to the guard. "Shoot it now, before the B gene regenerates." The guard wastes no time, instantly locking and loading. Aiming the gat with extreme precision, he shoots the caged fiend in the head, dead center. The helpless man trapped within the body of a beast reemerges, falling flat to the floor. His gray eyes settle back into their original chocolatey brown hue. Caleb leers uneasily at the expiring man, wondering what might have caused him to choose Akache. He watches as a pool of blood seeps out from the cage to the floor right beneath their feet. With the one last bit of strength he can muster, the man tilts his head, eyes locking on Caleb.

"Help us," the dying man begs. The next second, his movements come to a close. His eyes dim, the lids drop shut, and he passes on. All life once within him is gone. Fitz watches the warrior's quiet death with genuine surprise; it's hard to believe he's taken out one of the Akache.

"It worked! It worked!" Fitz exclaims. Meanwhile, Jaylen ignores the celebratory tone of Fitz's words. The teen drops to his knees, staring with sadness at the lifeless African American man whose life was stolen right before his eyes.

"I hope you are proud of what you just did," Jaylen states.

"These moments are never proud for me," Fitz replies. "This is science. Nothing can stand in the way of science — not even Akache." The scientist smiles to himself with glee over his most recent finding.

"I won't give you any more blood." Fitz's head whips around so fast, it looks like it just might spin off. Catching a glimpse of Caleb's confident grin, Fitz stammers, trying to get out his objection.

"You're not understanding. This is the single biggest find of the last century. You have a stake in this, Caleb. America needs you."

"You'll kill millions of African Americans if I give you more blood."

"Every war has collateral damage – and we aren't asking you for that much blood," Fitz expresses as convincingly as possible.

Off to the side, Jaylen stands quiet, unable to shake his focus from the man's lifeless body lying in the cage. The image triggers painful memories from his father's tragic murder. Finally, he surrenders, speaking a few words, more to himself than to anyone else.

"I've tried so hard to put it behind me," Jaylen starts. "But the moment I do, it's thrown back in my face. Maybe Karnitu is right… Maybe you all deserve death."

Fitz nonchalantly shoves his hands in his pockets. He stares down, admiring the dark maroon of the poor soul's blood as it gathers at his feet. "He gave his life in the name of science, boys. You shouldn't see it any other way. The President will be pleased at this vaccine. One vial of your blood will help save millions of lives. The two tankers following behind us carry fifty thousand doses of the shots. We will finally end this war and discover new worlds."

"You're sick," Jaylen snaps.

"No, I'm willing to save our country at any cost."

"Wait, did you just mention the President?" Caleb pipes up.

"Yes, he wants to see our new weapon in action."

"You idiot! You are leading Akache right to his doorstep."

"It's what they want. He has what they want."

"For such a young tot, you sure have a host of theories," Fitz quips. Suddenly, the tanker comes to a screeching halt, jostling the three of them.

"Fitz, it's too late," Caleb says in a foreboding tone.

The trio of tankers finally emerges from the tunnel, spit out into a dead end surrounded by mountains of greenery with no foreseeable exit. Hanging overhead is a brilliant array of cosmos. Twinkling stars light up the night sky. Headlights from the tanker cut through the heavy veil of darkness, revealing a prominent display ingrained within the pavement — the United States seal. Further ahead, a pair of towering doors are set within the mountain's outer wall. The pair of vaccine transport tankers bringing up the rear slowly come to a stop. The gargantuan metal monsters pull up side by side, taking up almost the entire space within the oval-shaped entryway. Fitz emerges from the leading tanker, forcing Micky, Caleb, and Jaylen out onto the pavement. Guards escort the group to the entry point where Doley awaits them with open arms.

"Finally," Doley exclaims, spitting out the toothpick between his lips. "We are going to get even with these bastards!" The sleazy advisor eyes the two colossal tankers. "The guns are there?"

"Yes, locked and loaded," Fitz affirms. "But keep in mind… I need a few of the aliens for research."

"No problem, Fitz. Just stay out of my way, and I'll stay out of yours." The two men shake on it.

"Where's the President?"

"He's inside, waiting on his weapons," Doley says, a deceptive smirk on his face. After a few moments, the concealed double doors slowly open with a screech. All of a sudden, a thunderous crack splits apart the sky. From out of the heavenly depths emerge one thousand Akache warriors, soaring downward with immense force. They land in droves atop each of the tankers, smashing through the thick metal coverings with ease. Caleb pulls away from Fitz, but the mad scientist refuses to loosen his grip.

"I told you," Caleb screams, frantically, practically in tears. "You led them here!" Hundreds of military soldiers pile out from the massive vehicles, guns loaded, firing the vaccine of death into the night. One by one Akache warriors fall from the sky, dropping like flies. Their muscular bodies plummet, kissing the cement, flailing on the ground as the poison seeps into their veins. Snipers obscured within the mountain wall reveal themselves, firing their weapons at the vaccinated fleet of alien creatures crumpled on the ground.

"Die, you fucking bastards! America first!" one of the soldiers screams as he lets loose a stream of bullets into the night. Without any warning, the camouflaged doors begin closing. Fitz, Micky, and the boys make a mad dash for safety, but something stops them in their tracks… A deafening cyclone forms, whirling about, blocking their way into the only entrance in sight. Wind funnels crop up, forcing everyone in the nearby vicinity to take cover. The vaccinated Akache warriors morph into their original human form for only a moment – before being brutally murdered by the soldiers.

"You're killing them. Stop it," Caleb screams with all his might. Despite the teen's plea, repeated gunfire lights up the sky.

From amid the swirling haze, the Akache commander, Karnitu, appears. The nefarious alien leader, weary and livid over the near eradication of his fleet, summons every bit of power he can gather within. With a single motion of his finger, he hoists the two transports high into the air. In one fell swoop, he flips over the tankers – they dangle in midair – and then slams them down to the ground, crushing them like tin cans.

"Aca mula condona!" Karnitu declares. Instantly, two miniature tornadoes materialize in the palm of his hands. The menacing invader puckers his lips, and with a single blow, the tornadoes transform into giant wind funnels that spiral toward the soldiers, swooping up everyone and anything in its path.

Doley and Fitz manage to evade the whirlwind's clutches and dart into the tunnel from where the tankers had just recently emerged. Karnitu glides ominously behind the two escapees, his will to destroy effortlessly goading him on.

Just outside the tunnel, hundreds of downed Akache warriors recover from their forced vaccination, and within five minutes, they're as good as new – except better. The warriors morph back from their original human form to their Akache form but one that's stronger, more powerful than ever before.

Meanwhile, the escape of Doley and Fitz isn't going as well as they had hoped. The faster the two run, the quicker Karnitu speeds along, catching up to them almost instantly. He grabs Fitz viciously by the neck, forcing Doley to bear witness to his brutally dominating power. Squeezing the scientist's throat with his thick fingers, the deranged commander utilizes Fitz as his surrogate for translation. The voice that leaves Fitz's mouth is one with a raspy inflection.

"Where is your leader?" Karnitu asks, speaking through Fitz. Doley takes off running to the end of the entrance, his fists banging relentlessly on a second pair of double doors.

"We've been breached! Let me in!" Doley screams through the metal doors. Karnitu lifts Fitz's fragile form into the air, exposing his soon-to-be-killed trophy to anyone who will turn his way.

The Akache army swarms the tunnel, pushing past Doley, knocking him flat on his ass. Calling on their otherworldly strength, the alien creatures pry open the monstrous metal doors with their bare hands. As soon as the doors open, bullets pour down, raining fire on the Akache. The warriors' metal shields and breastplates manage to deflect every shot that comes their way, protecting them for the time being.

Tightening his grip on Fitz's throat, Karnitu prompts the surrogate to speak once again. "Take me to your leader," Fitz croaks out.

The battle rages on as the Akache army moves in the opposite direction, next breaching the concealed mountain, easily overtaking the military. Suddenly infuriated at the rate of his army's progress, Karnitu tosses Fitz to the ground, watching for a moment as he wriggles away to safety… But of course, the vengeful commander won't let it end that pleasantly. Karnitu maliciously jams his foot onto Fitz's neck and plunges his spear right into his skull, killing him on the spot.

"Stop it!" Caleb screams, appearing behind the commander. "I know why you're here."

"Kahleo?"

"I'm not Kahleo. I'm Caleb." Karnitu approaches Caleb, gently caressing his jaw with his spindly fingers, taunting him. Repulsed by the unfortunate reunion, Caleb pulls away from the commander.

Outside of the mountain, one of the Akache warriors throws the First Lady to the ground. Suddenly, a panicked male voice sounds in the distance.

"Let her go! Let her go!" the voice shouts. The President emerges from the mountain next, restrained by two Akache warriors, spears held to his neck, piercing his tender flesh.

"You win! You win!" President Reid says, his hands raised in surrender. Whizzing out from the tunnel, Karnitu appears, grabbing the First Lady by the throat. He squeezes her throat tightly, eyeing the President with disdain.

"You have what I need. I'll spare her life if you hand it over."

"I don't know what you're talking about," President Reid answers, his words coming slowly, carefully as he tries his best to lighten up the intensity of the heart-pounding moment. Karnitu squeezes the First Lady's neck even tighter still. The pressure causes blood to trickle from her ears.

"No! No, leave her alone." The President falls to his knees, pleading, begging for his wife's safety with tears in his eyes. "Please, leave her alone. Okay, okay, I'll tell you."

The three teens stand off to the side, attempting to hide, watching the horror as it plays out before them.

"What are they talking about?" Jaylen asks Caleb. The boys keep their whispers to a minimum.

"That's what I've been trying to tell you, Jaylen. This was never about us, or the right to free us from bondage."

"Then, what is it about?" Jaylen asks. The boys go silent, intently watching, waiting for the President's next move. President Reid's troubled eyes dart back and forth, searching for something. Finally, his eyes land on Caleb, remorse guiding the following revelation.

"He's after the Fura Mukedu."

Chapter 19
The Fura Mukedu

The outlandish reality regarding the current state of the world has set in across the nation. Once all-encompassing, the red mist has dissipated from the atmosphere, exposing the evil Akache commander's devious plans. Within the green space just beyond the mountain, Karnitu finds himself in the midst of a standoff with the President's imposing military unit. The commander's ruthless grip clings tightly to the delicate skin of the First Lady's throat. Eyes rolling back in her head, the First Lady is steadily losing her life force. Karnitu continues using the fading woman as his surrogate, prompting her to relay his deplorable warnings to anyone within earshot.

"You could have saved millions of lives," the First Lady's voice croaks out, lacking the oxygen to rise much higher than a whisper. "But your planet will fall at the hands of my Akache regime. Every Belivian on your planet is finally waking up to the rampant destruction you've bestowed over their lives. I am here to save them, give them the purpose that they desire." Having heard enough of the commander's threats, Caleb steps into the limelight, ready to defend his people.

"You lie! You never wanted to help us… Only yourself." Karnitu sneers at the outspoken teen. He inhales a deep whiff of air.

"I smell fear, Kahleo."

"And I smell bullshit, commander. You used us for your own good. I just know it!" President Reid stands by, helplessly watching the verbal tennis match ensue between Caleb and the commander. He keeps his lips tight, allowing the petty exchange to go on. Caleb bravely shoves an accusing finger Karnitu's way.

"Yes, my people have suffered, but I'll be damned if I allow you to do any more harm to them," Caleb declares.

"And what are you going to do, Kahleo? Like the counterparts before you, you'll have to make a choice. It's the one commodity that your people should cherish most — choice."

"Yes, and I'm making the choice to see the truth for what it is," Caleb says, his responses growing more candid by the second. He uses his tiptoes to lift him as high as he can go, trying his best to make direct eye contact with the commander. Karnitu's grip around the First Lady's neck intensifies even more.

“All truths are self-blinding, while built on the lies of the powerful. Kahleo, most of your kind will ultimately see what they want to see.”

“I know what you are after, commander. It took me some time to piece things together.”

“If you know the truth, you know that power has no bounds.” All of a sudden, two African American soldiers sneak up behind Karnitu. They aim their rifles with precision and fire a round into the commander’s direction.

“Let her go, you sick fuck,” one of the soldiers shouts. Karnitu’s intense glare locked on Caleb never wavers, unconcerned by the dull threat from behind. A wicked smirk spreads across the alien leader’s tattooed mug. He discreetly opens the palm of one hand ever so slightly, and abruptly closes it. The simple gesture instantly crushes the two soldiers’ larynx. The men keel over in agony. They hit the ground hard as they claw at their throat, struggling to breathe, flailing to their death in a matter of seconds.

“That didn’t take long, commander,” Caleb says, unsurprised at the crude fatalities brought on by the Akache leader. “Your true colors are showing for the world to see.” The teen motions toward Jaylen, who's been broadcasting the live footage to the world.

Caleb speaks to the camera. "Black Americans, wake up! He was never for us. He's only here to silence us, give us a false sense of hope. I say we band together and rebuke Akache."

Just feet away, President Reid stands, listening intently to Caleb's fearless speech. Proud of his fellow American for taking a stand, the President adjusts his posture, holding his head high, despite the circumstances. He holds his breath, silently willing Caleb's words to have gotten through to the commander for once and for all. But nevertheless, Karnitu embarks on an alternate approach, vying to turn the tides back in his favor.

"Those two soldiers fought for a nation that persecuted every one of their freedoms. I set them free," Karnitu attests. As the commander speaks, harsh winds again come barreling through the space, letting loose a fury of chaos on everyone present. Jaylen's rage gets the better of him at this point, and so, he makes a beeline in front of Caleb, ready to face the commander. But once he and Karnitu are in a shared space, nearly toe to toe, the vocal teen loses his confidence, his mind reverting back to the shy little schoolboy he once was back in junior high.

"Commander, I want to believe what you are saying. I promise you, I do. But if 'choice' is our truth and the only way out of this debacle called 'America,' why hasn't our choice of freedom brought my people basic human rights?" Jaylen points at the two African Americans lying dead at his feet.

Jaylen kneels awkwardly, moving closer to the men, setting his head on one of their chests, listening for a heartbeat. The teen stealthily lifts the gun up and out of the fallen soldier's holster, stuffing it into his pants. Shaking his head sadly, Jaylen straightens up and faces the commander once again.

"They too had families that will never see them again. They too made a choice in the moment, and you chose to kill them at will. Your message is no better," Jaylen says, his words teeming with angst. "I wanted to align with your mission greatly, commander. But looking at all the death in the streets shook me to my core, no matter how hard I tried to suppress my guilt. We are not like you! I share your sentiment that a life without choice is death, but I denounce the way you're going about obtaining freedom. It has only ended badly."

"Well put, Jaylen," Caleb says, patting Jaylen on the back. Sensing that his plan has gone awry, Karnitu surveys the area — he's quickly losing his grip on the African American citizens, and he knows it. Suddenly, the commander decides to take matters into his own hands, snatching away Jaylen's phone and smashing it into pieces on the ground. A small group of cameras hover overhead, capturing the alien's hostage-like takeover.

"You have all been brainwashed," Karnitu screams up at them. "I am the only being that will set you free. Once the Fura Mukedu is in my power, you will no longer have to worry." A few feet away from the drama, Doley stands watching. He shifts closer to the President, whispering in his ear, digging for information.

"Mr. President, what is the Fura Mukedu?" Doley asks. President Reid urges him to hush, lowering his voice to a barely audible tone. While his voice quakes with trepidation, the desire to relinquish the top secret intel is overpowering, and he gives in.

"Only one living president at a time is privy to the Fura Mukedu…"

"I assumed it was a fable."

"No. And I shouldn't be telling you this, but under the circumstances, I have no other choice." Doley holds his breath, waiting for the President to continue. Meanwhile, the man in power hesitates, searching every last file in his mind for the most appropriate explanation. "The Library of Congress has a room. Only the living presidents are allowed in. I've never even been there. As President, during your first day in office, the letter your predecessor leaves is only about that room."

"So, the whole 'welcome to the White House' letter is bullshit?"

"Precisely. Only two living presidents can know about the confines of the room at a time."

"Former President Brannon died a few months ago… Which means you're the only one that has the information," Doley concludes. President Reid glances Karnitu's way, trying to avoid eye contact the best he can.

"I don't know how this monster knows, but he knows about the Fura Mukedu," the President states. Doley grows more anxious, tugging gently at the President's sleeve.

"But what is the Fura Mukedu?" Doley asks, but the President doesn't quite hear him – his eyes are glued to Karnitu, who squeezes his wife's neck tighter and tighter. Her life now truly hangs in the balance. Doley nudges him. "He's going to kill her, Mr.

President." President Reid regretfully turns away, a terrifying mixture of guilt, sorrow, and rage building up within him. But his realization is apparent and it shakes him to the core. What he knows is even more important than the survival of his wife.

Chapter 20
The Book of Diop

The last hour dragged by at the excruciating pace of a snail. High above the earth, over Camp David's spacious mountain opening, hovers the mothership of the Akache. The monstrous spacecraft covers the span of twenty football fields. Bright lights pummel downward from the sky, just as intrusive as the Akache brood itself, terrorizing the night with its daunting array of flashing bulbs. A group of Akache warriors aggressively escort President Reid and Doley toward the hypnotic light. The spears currently shoved into their spines prompt quicker strides from the two older men. Micky gets led into the light by two soldiers; she's starting to come back around by now. Caleb and Jaylen are the first to enter the ship, and they do so only because of the uncomfortable prodding from the warriors leading them into the otherworldly aura. Their teenage bodies effortlessly levitate just before being devoured by the metallic foreign spacecraft.

Karnitu prepares himself for ascension, absorbing the mystical white light shining from above. The commander's muscular frame freely glides upward toward the ship's opening. Following behind is the First Lady as her body reluctantly floats in midair.

As the woman ascends into the belly of the ship, a debilitating electrical charge overtakes her already fragile frame, crippling her instantly. The First Lady plunges downward, rapidly falling back toward Earth. President Reid, overtaken by sorrow, perks up slightly as he sees his wife once more – but then he notices the rate of her descent. The President flails with every ounce of strength, attempting to break free from the Akache warrior holding him back. More than anything, he wishes for the power to save his wife… But any and all attempts fail, and the only thing left for President Reid to do is watch helplessly as the love of his life collides with the ground.

The President does his best to keep it together as he and Doley stand underneath the circular gleam of illumination from overhead, dreading what events might follow. Their eyes shift to the surrounding Akache warriors, and then upward, peering at the massive extraterrestrial spacecraft. Then collectively, the feet of the only four white Americans in the immediate area – President Reid, the First Lady, Doley, and Micky separate from the ground, lifting them into the luminous glow.

As their bodies float higher and higher into the night sky, an enveloping, consuming electrical current races forth, slamming all four of them down to the ground. Four Akache warriors converge on the group of white Americans. The warriors wrap hulking arms around their weaker counterparts, restricting their movements. Instantly, the striking charge ignites once more, penetrating the white Americans' already immobile bodies. Screams of pain from the First Lady and Micky echo through the lonely night sky. The four pulverized bodies levitate, slicing their way through the glinting radiance of the ship's opening. With a resounding bang, the giant metallic door slams shut.

Once inside, President Reid and Doley take in every crevice, every alcove, every compartment within the ship's enormous interior. The view from afar doesn't do justice to the spectacular craftsmanship of the uniquely constructed ship.

Inside the massive spacecraft are long, sweeping corridors, only partially lit, with Akache warriors waiting at every turn. Caleb and Jaylen reluctantly follow behind the menacing commander, his oddly long strides making it difficult for them to keep up. Ancient writing covers every inch of the spacecraft's walls in a language that only the Akache can understand. Caleb stops periodically to examine the writing, trying to interpret it himself. Each time he stops, an overzealous Akache warrior lingers behind him, ready to prod him forward with a sharp poke of his spear. Armed with weapons, the inhospitable Akache patrolling the deck take a moment to observe their new visitors. Caleb and Jaylen take in the magnitude of the ship, surveying what the two teens silently deem as the 'floating Titanic.'

Probing the inner depths of his mind, Caleb struggles to recall the memories of his unpleasant time endured on this ship in the past. He sifts through the mental files as quickly as possible, hoping to drum up some idea of an escape route. The ship's structure is expansive, with several corridors leading to hidden rooms, secret compartments, and who knows what else. Eventually, the group reaches Karnitu's control room. A towering door slides open, allowing them entrance. The control room is where Karnitu leads his Akache force into battle. Inside is where the commander typically sits, atop his throne, consisting of a single bronze chair, molded into the shape of an 'A.' Sizable windows line the length of the circular-shaped room. The view provides a 360-degree look into the infinite universe — absolutely stunning.

Karnitu grabs the fragile body of the First Lady and effortlessly tosses her to the floor, hoping to provoke the President. The crude plan fails as the President remains silent, fully aware of his helplessness to change any aspect of the trauma before him. President Reid, Doley, and Micky get shoved to the floor just as quickly. A leftover stinging sensation pulses through their bodies, thanks to the electrical charges that recently coursed through their veins. Their bodies writhe around as the pain, growing worse with every moment, overtakes every inch of their body.

President Reid manages to fight through the anguish of his body long enough to crawl beside his wife, reuniting with his only love. Unable to move much, his lips gently caress her forehead, while she struggles to embrace him.

"Honey, it's going to be okay," President Reid whispers to his wife. The First Lady's limbs droop and she begins drifting in and out of consciousness. Weakness consumes her body, but she fights with all she can to keep her eyes from falling shut. She lovingly stares into her husband's oval face, the same way she did when they were high school sweethearts. Sensing the end is near, she mentally prepares as best as anyone can.

"I'll always love you, Adam," she whispers.

"I love you too. Honey, stay with me. Please." The First Lady smiles at her husband's futile sentiment – before being yanked from the floor by only her hair. Mercilessly, the commander's foot strikes the President in the chest, sending him sliding across the floor to the opposite end of the room.

"Leave my husband alone," the First Lady screams with as much power as she can muster, attempting to crawl over to her husband. Again, the First Lady's body is hoisted into air. She battles her heart out with Karnitu, hoping to free herself for even a single moment, but the powerful commander shoves his terrifying face into the woman's cheek. He summons a ring of smoke that escapes from his mouth. The mysterious smoke ring encircles the First Lady's body. Karnitu extends his vile black-colored tongue and caresses the woman's face seductively. The forced touch of the commander's tongue against her skin creates an unbearable burning sensation. She unleashes the most horrifying scream as the pain runs amok through her body. The devilish Karnitu smiles, basking with great pleasure in the woman's pain.

"Leave her alone, you hideous monster," President Reid says, spewing empty threats. A herd of intimidating Akache warriors report to the control room, encircling the Americans, positioning themselves for their most cruel battle yet.

The commander nonchalantly sneaks away to his control panel, jamming a few buttons in a particular sequence. One of the large windows sitting at the front of the room morphs into a digital screen, featuring images of various planets and galaxies. Karnitu motions to Caleb.

"Kahleo, these are the planets and galaxies of the unknown. I've conquered each of them without the Fura Mukedu." Caleb perks up, too intrigued to ignore the barbaric commander's words. He walks closer, his attention fastened on the screen as it veers into the expanding universe. Mesmerized by the vibrant colors and massive sizing of each of the incredible rotating planets, Caleb's eyes follow the lively hue saturating the depths of the universe, unable to break his gaze.

"How old are those planets?" Caleb asks, prompting Karnitu to grab firmly on to the First Lady's already crushed neck.

"Too old to quantify," the woman weakly states.

"Is that your home planet?"

"Akache is the dominant force in the eastern, southern, and western imperials. My forces have crushed all of those that challenged my reign. There is one imperial remaining."

Caleb's mouth drops, gawking at the commander. "The northern imperial. What makes you think you can conquer it?"

"My son, Akache's conquest to live in infinity goes through the northern imperial. My powers can't extend beyond the northern imperial until— "

Caleb interrupts, happy to challenge the commander's assertions. "Until you have the Fura Mukedu."

"The Fura— " the First Lady croaks, her voice growing weaker with each word, more airy by the second. The unrelenting commander just squeezes her neck tighter, urging her to speak louder. "The Fura Mukedu was once within reach, but your brother kept me from reaching its power."

"My brother? I don't have a brother," Caleb counters Karnitu's assertion, a confused smirk on his face.

"Kahleo, to know the world is to know thyself. The universe is your family. It is ready to welcome and nurture your presence. The quest remains – will you accept the call?" Caleb ignores the commander's question for the time being, his eyes still glued to the massive screen as it explores the confines of the universe.

"We only want peace, commander," Caleb says. Karnitu rises from his throne, sending a scowl of great displeasure down on the teen.

"You fool! They won't allow peace to you or the Belivian people. Your lineage is too strong to remain dormant. You were created to conquer all those who condemn your existence."

Finally breaking away his attention from the screen, Caleb sticks a hand out to President Reid, helping him rise from the floor. Watching in shock, Karnitu points an accusing finger the teen's way.

"You are a trader to your own race, Kahleo."

"Caleb," Jaylen pipes up, "I think we better do something fast. You're making him angry." The anxious teen quickly jumps away from the commander's throne. Hands falling to his side, Caleb holds his head high, confidence somehow racing through his entire body.

"I'm willing to fight for truth and peace, commander."

"No, Kahleo, you're fighting for a choice that has been chosen specifically for you and the Belivians."

"Lies!" Caleb says, nearly spitting in the commander's face.

"Your fight is an illusion, one that will never end, because Belivians take pleasure in being treated like subjects. It excites you, brings you profound fulfillment. Pathetic," Karnitu spouts with defiance.

The teen does a quick scan of the room, taking note of the Akache brigade encircling the room. As he eyes the creatures, he sees them for who they really are deep down inside – or at least, who they were. Caleb recognizes a few gang members and some students he's known since high school. Realizing it's likely too late for them, Caleb's heart breaks as he comes to terms with the various lies Karnitu has conjured up. Life-changing lies, all to rally Black Americans for their willing participation in his cruel, inhumane war.

"I get it now," Caleb resumes. "You don't have the power. You need us, Black Americans, to reach the Fura Mukedu. Your fleet's power isn't strong enough." The commander allows a few tense moments to pass while Caleb pieces together his thoughts. "Why didn't I think of this before? It all makes sense."

"Yeah, Cal, these bastards did what America has always done… Used our adversity against us. Making us think they are in our corner, while plotting against us the entire time." Jaylen backs up his friend, sidling next to him – they're in this fight together, from beginning to end. Karnitu unveils a most haunting smirk, deviously gazing down at the teens.

"You are building an army to capture the Fura Mukedu," Caleb declares his realization.

Jaylen tugs at his friend's arm, whispering into his ear. "Again, what is the Fura Mukedu?"

Karnitu lifts to his feet and saunters over to the screen. All eyes are on him. "The Fura Mukedu is the envy of the universe, the nucleus that creates life in the universe. The commander pauses in thought, staring at the planets rotating on the screen before stepping away. He motions to his warriors. "Bring their leader to me." The Akache warriors ruthlessly grab the President, once again throwing him down to the floor. Karnitu stares down judgmentally at him. "This is your precious leader?"

"Go fuck yourself!" President Reid exclaims, in between catching his breath.

"Where is the Fura Mukedu?" Karnitu asks, getting in the President's face.

"I'll never tell you! You are pure evil."

"No, Mr. President. That, I am not. You are a disgrace to your own people. You sold one million of your people to me. You are undoubtedly more sinful than I. How can you be followed by so many but offer so little fight and intelligence?"

"You tricked us into believing you cared about our world," the President replies. Karnitu slams the tip of his spear into the ground.

"Silence! You have no idea what you're up against. I'm going to ask you again. Where is the Fura Mukedu?"

"And I'll say it again," President Reid begins, "go fuck yourself, commander." A crippling silence falls over the room.

Karnitu takes a moment, pondering all the ways in which he could potentially extract his desired information from the President. The demented commander tosses the First Lady to the floor once again. He makes one swift motion to the fleet, and they approach the President, aggressively ushering him toward the commander. Karnitu's giant form ominously towers over the six-foot-tall

President, staring down at him with a look of vengeful hostility. President Reid lifts his fist to his face, preparing to do battle for his other love — his country. Caleb and Jaylen watch from the side, doing their best to keep a lid on their emotions but secretly respecting the President's vigor.

"You are a mere swindler who sold your people into the great slave trade," Karnitu states. Catching sight of the teens' brown faces, the President's eyes water, suddenly overcome with emotion.

"And I am willing to die for my people," President Reid declares.

"No, Mr. President! Don't do this," Doley announces, backing himself into a corner.

"I've killed plenty of cowards like you," the commander says, "exposing them for the weaklings they were. But not one of them had betrayed their people like you have."

"Are you going to stand there and talk, or are we going to get to it, commander?"

"Honey, please don't do this," the First Lady mumbles under her breath. Her pulverized body remains lifeless on the cold, hard floor. Karnitu watches the President adoring his wife from afar. All of the human emotion nauseates him. He grips the throat of the First Lady one final time.

"It's the single reason you'll die here – emotion. Your human emotions have altered your mental capacity to decipher choice versus truth. Looking past your emotions would bring you strength, power, and longevity as a nation." Karnitu parades around the room like a deranged professor teaching a class that should never be taught. He creeps up from behind, pushing the First Lady's lips to the President's ear. She emits a terrifying whisper.

"Death is the only option to counter indecisiveness on my planets. It's knocking at your soul, Mr. President. You've brought the fight here; not I."

"Just leave us alone."

"I'm repulsed by the lies you've told your people. I'm convinced that millions of Belivians will die at your hands," Karnitu taunts. Jaylen's angry streak suddenly returns. He gives the President the side-eye.

"He's right, President Reid," the teen starts. "The Melanin Experiment was a failed policy and cost Black lives." The President turns to the boys. His voice cracks with every syllable.

"Don't believe him. He's lying. He's a mass manipulator with an agenda. I wanted to try and save lives, and nothing more.

You've got to believe me," President Reid says, pleading, desperation in his eyes.

Jaylen swings around to look at Karnitu, then back to the President. He wears a discouraging look on his face, processing the alleged statements from both sides, struggling to lean one way or the other. Caleb takes a few steps back from the commander and instead nears the President.

"Is he telling the truth about the Fura Mukedu?" Caleb asks. For years, the President has kept mum on the subject of the Fura Mukedu – but now, he's ready to talk. The room once again goes silent.

"This monster is correct," President Reid says. "Since the country's inception, there have been talks about the Fura. Most historians deemed it a falsehood contrived by the French. I, too, assumed it was a fable. I have never studied the authenticity of the legend of Fura Mukedu. There's a book." Caleb and Jaylen hang onto the President's every word, listening with such intensity as if being told a spooky story around a campfire.

"The historical document is called, The Book of Diop, which has been guarded by the four disciples. Each distinct 'Diop' represents historic offerings by the unknown imperial of our universe. Historians deemed it a hoax for centuries, as did I… Until I saw the writings with my own eyes. The unmitigated truth is beyond anyone's imagination. I still don't believe what's in that book. But if the Book of Diop is true, then I can understand why you would want the Fura Mukedu." President Reid turns back to Karnitu. He loosens his tie, a huge weight having been lifted from his conscious. His body eases into a state of relaxation, as much as is possible, given the circumstances.

"I can take you to the book, which would tell you where the Fura Mukedu resides."

"Where is it?" Karnitu demands. The President hesitates, realizing that once the information is out there, it's out there for good – no turning back.

"The Library. The Library of Congress," President Reid says with finality.

Karnitu hoists his spear victoriously into the sky. Every Akache warrior in the room joins in on the movement, lifting their spears high into the air and chanting vigorously in their native tongue. "Aca sula Fura Mukedu! Aca sula Fura Mukedu!"

Jaylen leans into Caleb, muttering under his breath. "He said all of that and I still don't know what the hell the Fura Mukedu is... And the four disciples?! I thought there were twelve."

“Looks like the book provides the coordinates to the Fura Mukedu,” Caleb answers absently. The boys are suddenly joined by Micky, who tends to her ailments the best she can. She runs over and huddles close to them.

“Guys, something isn't right. I've read the historical documents about the Book of Diop in junior high. It never said anything about the Library of Congress or the Fura Mukedu.”

“So, you think the President is lying?” Caleb whispers.

“I don't know. But the book has been strategically placed somewhere on the East Coast, and presumably hidden for a reason. My guide in Africa never mentioned a Fura Mukedu. There are a slew of documents in African that support what I am proposing, but they are hidden in caves near the edge of Ghana. I spoke to a woman once; she was a Nganga. She led our excursion into the country.”

“Nganga?” Jaylen asks, a confused look on his face.

“Yes, they are considered pupils of immense wisdom in Africa,” Micky replies. Now, Jaylen has heard it all. He turns his back to Micky, pausing in thought for a moment.

"Then, the faster we get these creeps the Fura Mukedu, the quicker they can leave our planet," the hopeful teen says. Micky and Caleb share a look of unease as they stare into the distance, already knowing that the President's revelation is only the beginning.

Jaylen continues. "Guys, all they want is this Fura bullshit. I say we help them find it, and I can finally get back to enjoying my fantasy football."

"Unfortunately, Jaylen, this may be more complex than we realized."

"How so?!" Jaylen asks. Micky pulls him close, attempting to reel him in from further off-the-cuff questioning.

"You're not getting it," Micky continues as delicately as she can. "They desperately need the Book of Diop, which will point them in the direction of the Fura Mukedu. This can't be good…" Angst echoes in her truthful words. From behind the huddled teens, Doley secretly retrieves a red gun from his pocket and points it at the commander.

"It's over, commander," Doley shouts. "Go to hell!" Immediately, Doley pulls the trigger, nailing the bullet right into the commander's neck. But the slug manages to lodge itself into Karnitu's throat before having a chance to dissolve into its liquid form. The poisonous fluid begins spreading through the evil invader's body, quickly reaching his heart. He swings around with speed, hurling his arms into the air, summoning his most extraordinary powers…

But then it happens – his powers stall and his legs buckle, bringing him down to his knees. The commander's body vibrates uncontrollably, sending him flat to the ground. The alien's once impressive muscles recede, leaving behind nothing more than a bony mass of flesh. The intricate designs covering the commander's body all dissipate, reverting his immaculate red skin back to its original hue, a pristine, solid chocolate.

The surrounding Akache warriors watch in silent shock as their beloved leader completes his transformation back to the original smaller, weaker version of himself. Paying homage to their fallen commander, the warriors kneel before the true Karnitu. The heinous need to fight, maim, and destroy simmers briefly as the warriors lower their heads, closing their almond-shaped eyes for a meaningful moment of silence. Soft chants from the warriors flit around the room. "Aca sula Karnitu. Aca sula Karnitu."

Suddenly, Caleb collapses to one knee as his body mirrors the same painful sensation being felt by the commander. The uncomfortable feeling of a gunshot wound absorbs and pulses through the teen's body, with a will of its own. An excruciating throbbing settles into his chest, overpowering him. It brings him down to both knees, keeling over in horrific distress. Caleb's thunderous yelps of agony flood the expansive room, frightening Micky.

"Caleb, don't do this now," she says. Behind her, Jaylen pulls a gun from his pocket. He proceeds to point it at the leaderless Akache warriors as they yield to the weapon. Then he swings around, aiming right at Karnitu.

"Kill him!" President Reid screams his heart out. "Kill him now! We don't have time. He'll convert back." Jaylen's heart races. He concentrates on the President's words, targeting the commander with the gun he snagged previously from the fallen soldier on the mountain. President Reid forces a pleading gaze Jaylen's way. "If you want to save humanity, Jaylen, you'll kill him now!"

Jaylen tenses up. The intensity of the situation is becoming too much for him. He turns, watching Caleb fight for his life, writhing in pain on the ground. The violent movement startles him. Caleb slowly does his best to roll over, barely able to make eye contact with his friend.

"Shoot him, Jaylen," Caleb manages to gets out.

"But I'm afraid it would kill you, Caleb."

"It's okay, Jaylen. You can end this now."

President Reid's tone heightens even further. His eye is intently set on the watch around his wrist. "Shoot him! I'm begging you. We only have one minute left."

Jaylen's finger nervously shakes on the trigger. His mind becomes foggy as nerves get the best of him. The confused teen pivots, suddenly pointing the barrel at the President, then at Doley, before finally settling on Karnitu once more. He peers down at Caleb, fighting not to tear up. The terrified boy knows that pulling the trigger will mean instant death for his best friend in the world. But nevertheless, the President's grim words ring his ears, urging him to make his single most important decision yet, one that will undoubtedly change life forever. He closes his eyes, taking a much-needed breath. Jaylen pulls the trigger.

Chapter 21
The Library of Congress

Unquenchable fires now rage on across state lines throughout America. An explosive race war has broken out in some of the most densely populated cities in the country. Some of the smaller cities, especially those that are predominantly white, are burning to the ground as countless looters and rioters take to the streets. The latest headline in the news regarding the galactic violence reads, "The Akache War: Every race for itself." Akache warriors invade cities, converting them into recruitment centers designed for incoming aspirants. Nearly every street corner is set up with Asian, Hispanic, and American-run shops, each selling their own version of shirts, flags, buttons, and pins. The main commonality is the text – "I survived Akache."

Approximately half of the entire African American population has sworn to stick to their guns, further uniting themselves as a race by joining the Akache regime. They hope that their sacrifice will help rid the world of systemic racism. Meanwhile, the remaining percentage of African Americans vow to fight alongside the United States. They parade the streets in protest of the Akache invasion, holding signs that say, "We are not for sale. Black to Black matters. Say no to the Akache War."

Global allies still insist upon keeping their distance, choosing to watch the divisive war on their televisions instead, hiding away in the safety of their living rooms. A vast majority of the world as a whole are rooting for the Akache, hoping that they will conquer the United States for once and for all. Others fill their time by holding memorials, considering it their duty to not let the ongoing deaths throughout the country go unnoticed. For decades, foreign countries across the globe have viewed America as the "bully on the hill." Thanks to the contentious relationships they've presented countless times to the global community, America has lost out big-time, with every last one of their allies choosing to stay uninvolved. They offer up no help whatsoever, their only job being to sit back and watch the implosion of America.

For the first time in the history of the United States, legislation on reparations has been brought to the table, as well as an extensive stimulus package to help slightly ease the ongoing race relations ensuing around the country. For many African Americans, though, it's a little too late — instead, they are choosing to join the Akache regime in droves. These newly transformed Akache warriors are responsible for hunting down members of Congress, extinguishing them in any way they see fit.

After the two vaccine transport tankers were destroyed, Science and Technology worked for days on end, managing to harvest a menial number of the Akache transformation vaccine. These emergency doses are hard to come by, and they have already been distributed throughout the military. The National Guard finds it increasingly difficult to fend off the ever-expanding Akache fleet. The more battles, the more African Americans become one with the menacing species.

Deep in the heavens overhead, the expansive Akache mothership glides across the sky, maintaining an oddly sluggish pace. Inside the spacecraft, President Reid pleads with Jaylen, screaming in desperation.

"Jaylen, shoot him now!" President Reid screams once more. A weakened Karnitu slowly peers up into the barrel of the gun. As the vaccine's effect wears off, the commander's inhuman strength begins to make its return. Just then, Doley races up behind Jaylen, tackling the teen like a linebacker. Doley struggles to loosen the gun from Jaylen's death grip but the teen refuses to give up control of the weapon.

"No, don't!" Jaylen screams to Doley. "If we kill him, we kill my friend!" The two tussle on the floor. All of a sudden, a sharp bang resounds through the spacious room. Everyone gasps, some taking cover. The room settles, watching the devastating moment going on before their eyes. Doley's sagging, bloated form rests unmoving atop Jaylen's lanky body. The conniving advisor stares down into the teen's brown face.

"You shot me," Doley announces. A painful sensation begins its trek toward his spine. Jaylen shoves the advisor's tubby body off of him. Doley flops to the floor.

Once free from the weight of the man's fat, Jaylen rises at the speed of light, pointing the gun directly at Karnitu. But his hands shake uncontrollably as he clutches the hefty weapon, a feeling of unease washing over him. Specks of Doley's blood stain the teen's face. Wiping it away from his eye, Jaylen adjusts his feet in place, using every bit of his inner strength to keep his nerves under control. He's never fired a gun before, and the rush of both excitement and fear puts him on edge. Out of the corner of his eye, Jaylen notices Caleb. He looks to be regaining some of his strength, or so Jaylen thinks. The teen gently nudges his friend with the toe of his shoe, but Caleb doesn't come to as quickly as hoped.

Doley manages to prop himself up against one of the walls off to the side. Sitting on his bum, the sneaky man tries inhaling oxygen at a fast rate, expecting the air to somehow reenergize his body. He wraps both hands around his abdominal wound, restricting the blood freely pouring out from the gunshot. Little does the advisor know, the oozing plasma continues to seep out, dribbling a trail around his hands, down his leg, and onto the floor.

Doley loses consciousness rather quickly after that, but true to form, he manages to croak out some final demands along the way. "Shoot him, you idiot! Shoot him."

The vaccine nearly having worn off by now, Karnitu summons the strength to will his red cape to cloak his entire body, wrapping him up like a mummy for protection while his body regenerates. Soon after, the threatening Akache leader returns to his original prominence. His scrawny African American exterior morphs back into his powerful, ripped alien physique. The intricate designs begin returning to their places along his face and body. The commander's fangs return, sharper than before. The enchanted cape unfastens itself, its work done. The red fabric falls away from Karnitu's body, revealing the new, improved, even more fierce leader.

President Reid watches in distress. He's well aware that the one chance to wipe out Karnitu and his band of fiends has slipped away. The commander stands, his strength anew, towering over Jaylen. The teen can't help but examine the new upgrades made to Karnitu's buff exterior. Even the undecipherable markings on the alien's muscular frame are more mesmerizing than ever. Jaylen still clutches the gun, but it slowly dips down to his side.

"I can't do it," Jaylen says, defeated. "I just can't do it."

Doley sighs from his spots against the wall, letting loose a much-needed exhale. He whispers fearfully to himself. "God bless us all."

The beastly commander casually strolls over to Doley, hoisting him high into the air with an iron grip. Helpless, Doley's body forcefully slides up the wall of the corridor. Karnitu clasps a meaty hand around the advisor's neck, summoning an even tighter clench. Using Doley as a surrogate, the commander unleashes his next spew of cruel verbal affirmations.

"You're going to die. Akache is the way, the light, the conquerer. Anyone desiring a life force from this point must contend with Akache." Karnitu forces the advisor downward. Doley's feet scrape along the floor as the commander parades his current victim in front of Jaylen.

"My son, I've traveled billions of your Earth years, contemplating why the Belivian race had lost its passion to conquer mediocrity. The Palecians are the enemy; not I." Karnitu's hypnotic speech draws Jaylen forward. The gun slips free from the teen's hand, smashing to the floor. "Join me, Belivian, and I shall set you free."

"He's a liar. Get away from him," the President of the United States bravely declares. Karnitu shoves Doley to the floor, his sights now set on the one and only President Reid. Jaylen seizes his chance, ready to make things right with Doley.

"You'll be dead in the morning," Jaylen whispers in the defeated advisor's ear before walking away, leaving him cowering on the floor. The kneeling Akache warriors suddenly perk up, delighted by their leader's resurgence. Gradually, the warriors lift from their knees, anxiously preparing for their next task. The vengeful Karnitu grabs the President by the throat.

"Aca mesa cua Fura Mukedu."

"I'll never tell you! Go to hell!" President Reid states with vigor. The devious commander calmly takes in the President's insults, digesting them for a long moment. Then in a split second, he plunges the sharp end of his spear deep into the President's leg. An overwhelming screech echoes through the corridor, growing louder and louder as Karnitu gives the sharp object embedded within President Reid's thigh a few hearty twists. The commander regrets nothing, staring into the President's eyes with pure hatred as he mangles the man's limb.

"Aca mesa cua Fura Mukedu!" Karnitu chants. The commotion is enough to awaken the barely conscious First Lady. She lifts her head off the floor, just barely, and makes eye contact with her husband.

"Adam, please tell him. He'll kill you," the woman pleads. With that, the commander forces the piercing object even further into the President's leg. The most frightening scream yet pours from President Reid's mouth, startling Jaylen, paralyzing the teen in place. Again, the First Lady begs. "Please, Adam, tell him!" The President flails loosely, all the strength draining from his body as blood pours down his pant leg. He tries his hardest to maintain composure but the pain has crossed over into unbearable territory. Beads of sweat race one another as they roll down the President's beet red oval face. Out of the corner of his eye, he can see his wife's broken body on the floor. He gets lost in the traumatizing imagery, finally arriving at a decision.

"Okay! I'll take you," President Reid shouts, surrendering to the commander. "Please take it out! I'll take you to the Fura Mukedu." A haunting grin of triumph spreads across Karnitu's face. Rolling his compassionless eyes, he roughly yanks the spear free from the President's leg.

The next moment, President Reid's body hits the floor with a bang, his wound currently unable to maintain the pressure of standing. Jaylen hurries over, removing the President's tie from around his neck and bounding it tightly around the injured leg.

"I'll give you the coordinates to where the Book of Diop is… Inside, you'll find the location for the Fura Mukedu. Just leave us alone…" President Reid says to the commander, drifting in and out of consciousness.

An hour has since passed. The behemoth Akache mothership hovers no more than thirty feet above the entrance to the

United States Capitol. A red mist vigorously emerges from the ship's exterior, flowing through the air, saturating the atmosphere. Without any warning, neither light nor sound, a massive ramp peels open from the entrance of the ship, lowering all the way down to the ground. An impressive army of Akache warriors march downward in unison from the ship, to the entrance of each federal building accessible on the grounds. The sea of warriors patrol the deserted estate, patiently awaiting their next instructions. Nosy reporters have planted themselves on the nearby building rooftops, stealthily capturing live photos of the historic event taking place right before their eyes.

Jaylen and Micky carefully guide the ailing President on his descent from the mouth of the spacecraft. By this point, Caleb has fully regained his strength, but nevertheless, he is sure to keep a few paces between himself and Karnitu as they approach the Library of Congress. After climbing the mountain of steps, they reach a pair of double doors leading to the entrance.

The aggressive Akache warriors are the first to enter the building, spears raised, ready for battle – but they find no imminent danger. Seconds later, President Reid and the teens walk in, entering the tremendous foyer;

it's simply breathtaking. The wall-to-wall marble floors are stunning, with soaring pillars lining the expansive space. Statues of former presidents adorn either side of the room. Karnitu glides into the foyer behind the rest, his patience wearing quite thin at the moment.

"Aca cua the Fura Mukedu?" the commander bellows.

"What is he saying?" Micky whispers to Jaylen. Caleb turns to the President.

"He wants to know where the Fura Mukedu is." With Micky's help, President Reid wobbles further into the room, stopping at the actual entrance to the famous Library.

"It's through here," the President says before pushing open a pair of golden doors that lead into the overwhelmingly cavernous book-filled room, the Library of Congress.

Caleb and Jaylen make their way to the front of the group, admiring the millions and millions of books perched on immaculately organized shelves. Jaylen stumbles toward the center of the immediate area, doing a 360, taking in a panoramic view of the historic structure's beauty.

"Whoa, that's a gang of books," Jaylen says in awe at the sweeping staircases, fifty-foot ceilings, and exhaustive amount of books filling the landmark. "Why would the Fura Mukedu be here?"

"Quiet," President Reid says in a hushed tone, turning to the teens, "or else he'll hear you." The legion of Akache warriors blow past the President just then, leaping effortlessly from floor to floor. Even more warriors join in, swarming the stairs, marching with purpose to the second, third, and fourth floors. Soon enough, the entire library is flooded with Akache forces. The vengeful aliens turn over tables, hurl bookcases, and tear down renowned artwork from the walls. The combative fleet has taken matters into their own hands, surveying each and every floor in search of the Fura Mukedu.

"Aca cua the Fura Mukedu?" Karnitu yells from his place on the first floor.

"It's up there," President Reid shouts, pointing toward the uppermost floor. The tormenting commander suddenly grabs for the President's collar. With Karnitu's superhuman strength, he uses the tuft of material within his claws to effortlessly levitate the President's body higher and higher until reaching the fourth floor. Caleb darts up the staircase, snaking his way through the countless stone-faced warriors, his eyes locked on one thing only: Karnitu. Downstairs, the warriors swarm Jaylen and

Micky, forcing them to stay put. Caleb finishes zigzagging up the winding staircase, having made it to the fourth floor. The teen crouches down next to President Reid, who has since fallen to his knees, his strength depleting more and more with each passing second.

"We must go down that hall… And up a second set of stairs," the President murmurs. Caleb helps the weary man to his feet, pulling him through the hall. Every single corridor they reach is lined with Akache, their heads erect, their weapons perched for battle. Caleb and the President scurry down a hall before reaching a final staircase. The two climb the steps.

"Why would this Fura Mukedu be hidden here? A library?" Caleb asks.

"Shhhhh," President Reid says, placing an index finger up to his own lips. Finally, they reach the hidden floor. A solid metal door waits at the very top of the staircase, bright red "WRONG WAY" signage embedded within it. Next to the door sits a digital PIN pad. The feeble President probes his mind for the correct combination. Karnitu steps up behind him, jabbing his dangerous spear into the President's shoulder, urging him along. A moment later, the President nervously taps in a sequence of numbers –

he breathes a sigh of relief as the door unlocks, clicking open.

Through the door, an elevator awaits. President Reid, Caleb, and Karnitu step into the dangling metal box. As the doors smash closed, Caleb and the President congregate on the right end of the elevator, while Karnitu positions himself on the opposite side. On the digital console, Caleb notes four numbers.

"We need to go to the fifth floor," the President states, nursing his injured thigh.

"There is no five," Caleb answers with a confused tilt of the head. President Reid's eyes wince closed. He feels it; the pain in his leg is taking over. The suffering man sinks his teeth into his lower lip, trying hard to hold in his scream. Heavy breathing soon follows.

"Press all four buttons, Caleb." Heeding the President's instruction, Caleb sticks out his index finger, using it to illuminate each number one by one. After all four numbers are lit, the elevator begins to move, creeping upward. The irritating grind of rusty elevator cables in desperate need of oil breaks through the awkward silence. Soon, the doors separate, revealing a small oval-shaped room.

The space is no bigger than a typical studio apartment, with just enough space for up to four people or so to move around comfortably. The room's decor is minimal, with only a few dated pieces of furniture spread throughout the room. An assortment of antique books collecting dust sits on shelves lining the walls of the quaint space. Both Karnitu and Caleb step into the room with caution, examining the area with uncertainty.

The room is essentially a windowless box, with no escape to the outside world, and the air is thinning, provoking a hearty cough from the teen. Two tiny wall-mounted lamps provide the only illumination available in the dimly lit quarters. Set right in the middle of the room is a work table bearing a resemblance to the Resolute desk. Based on the spiderwebs engulfing the bookshelves and desk, this room looks to have gone untouched for years at a time. Curiosity getting the best of the teen, Caleb circles the room, eyeing the titleless books arranged on the shelves.

"What are these books?" Caleb asks. President Reid keeps a vigilant eye on Karnitu, who seems to enjoy stalking him from behind. He does his best to provide an answer.

"Each of those books are classified. Only the acting President of the United States has clearance here."

"Aca cua the Fura Mukedu?" Karnitu asks with a loud bark. The President fumbles through the massive collection of books, knocking some to the floor, frantically searching for the precise manuscript.

"It's got to be here," President Reid says, still rifling through the stacks. Caleb tugs on his suit jacket.

"Wait, you don't know what the book looks like?" Caleb asks in a low tone.

"No. No president does. There was never a moment that called for it."

By now, every last one of the bookshelves in the oval-shaped room has been wiped clear. They stand nearly empty. Documents, classified readings, and various other files cover the floor. Historic documents that have never once seen the light of day are thrown into a careless heap down below. Caleb's eyes widen as he gazes around the room, catching glimpses of candid photos featuring the likes of Martin Luther King, Gandhi, and even Hitler.

"It's got to be here somewhere," the President says, desperately searching through each and every book while kneeling on the hard floor. An indentation in the third shelf suddenly catches Caleb's eye.

"What's that?" Caleb asks, helping President Reid up from his spot on the floor. They climb over mountains of books. Finally reaching the shelf, the two share a look and then a nod as they realize that what they've been looking for is sitting right in front of them. The President carefully peers over his shoulder, checking on Karnitu's positioning.

Resting inside the shelf is a digital screen, big enough for a handprint. President Reid had heard about a 'secret room' through the years, but never once did he imagine that it could be the gateway to saving humanity. He sets his bare hand onto the digital glass panel. The screen initializes, calibrating for a moment before scanning the identifying creases embedded within the President's hand. All of a sudden, a panel of shelving slides open, unveiling a podium with a single book encased in glass.

"That's it, Mr. President," Caleb murmurs. The President acts promptly, tying his jacket around his fist, using it to break through the case. Glass shatters into countless pieces, exposing the book to air for the first time in who knows how long

The fierce commander shoves President Reid to the side, snatching the book right out of his reach. Karnitu goes to open the book – but it doesn't budge. A devilish frown, one filled with the utmost rage, cements itself into the commander's face. His fists clench, holding onto nothing for dear life. Then the commander unleashes a most horrifying squeal, one that couldn't possibly quantify as a language of any kind.

"Aca kaun sulu na!" Karnitu flings the ancient book into the nearest wall and immediately charges toward both President Reid and Caleb, who stare back in horror.

Chapter 22
The Day That Reckoned

Dawn collides with dusk, beams of the sun's powerful rays glare through the windows of the usually peaceful Library of Congress. Thousands upon thousands of Akache warriors surround the historic building, barring the vast military personnel attempting to contest the war that Akache has clearly already won. The United States military lingers near the front of the building, but regardless of any ploys, weapons, or riot gear, they are no match for the beastly attacks brought on by the Akache warriors. Leaping downward from hundreds of feet in the air, the acrobatic warriors relentlessly slam down their prey one by one, pouncing like starving leopards in the night.

The most recent leg of the intense battle has raged on for the better part of an hour. The more military deployed, the more troops killed. The hostile warriors use their invincible combat skills to defeat the influx of military assailants, majestically soaring through the air above, docking on military tankers, and ripping them open with their bare hands. Bodies of innumerable American soldiers get flung from one end of the sky to the other, pulverizing them into lifeless hunks of blood and guts.

A squadron of Akache ships hover overhead in the sky, spraying down a light coating of their signature red mist. The vibrant cherry-colored haze instantly penetrates through the flesh of every warrior below, each of them stopping to inhale the mist through their uniquely-shaped nostrils. Once inhaled, the mist acts as a strengthening agent for the warriors. Their eyes widen and their necks grow, thickening up a few inches. The exquisite red shade of their exterior gleams brighter than ever before, highlighting their well-defined back and arm muscles.

The enhanced powers of the Akache warriors are a treat to watch — if not for the fact that using them means destroying every American unlucky enough to be in their warpath. They hurl American soldiers effortlessly into the air like rag dolls. The warriors throw their spears like javelin sticks, sending them hundreds of yards in a matter of seconds. Flares from an onslaught of military gunfire light up the night sky. Invasive sparks slice through the Akache mist, heading straight for the backs of the warriors — but as indestructible as ever, the ammo simply bounces off of the creatures' glossy bodies.

A helicopter hovers overhead, ensuring a comfortable distance between them and those involved within the hopeless battle. Coming from the aircraft is a blinding spotlight encircling the building.

Back inside the Library of Congress, there is a hidden room located on the little-known fifth floor in the building. Within the room, Karnitu lunges at the President, his elongated fingers wrapping around the larynx of the "most powerful man in the world." President Reid's skull bashes violently against the wall, leaving behind a miniature crater. With that, the older man's limbs sag, the remaining fight left in him quickly slipping away.

Caleb rolls away to safety. Kneeling, the quick-witted teen rummages through the massive piles of books, moving with as much speed as he can. He tosses book after book to the side, struggling to locate the right one. With his back facing Karnitu, Caleb does his best to keep tabs on the commander, obsessively glancing over his shoulder. The thought of the commander releasing his unearthly wrath behind his back, without even a fighting chance, horrifies the teen.

"There it is," Caleb proclaims with a soft cry under his breath. The ancient book remains in pristine condition, with the words The Book of Diop embroidered on its cover. Sounds from a helicopter hovering overhead needles at the teen's eardrums. He listens closely for a moment, silently contemplating the potential help that could be waiting just outside the building.

Caleb returns from his thoughts, swinging around just in time to see Karnitu drag President Reid into the waiting elevator. He stuffs the book into his pants and races for the elevator. But it's too late — the heavy metal door slides shut with a clunk. With no time to waste, Caleb bangs on the door, his open palm repeatedly making contact with the cool metal, thudding over and over.

"Commander! Commander!" Caleb screams desperately.

A few short minutes later, the door slides open, allowing Caleb's entrance into the empty elevator. "Where did they go?" He steps inside and presses the button for the ground floor.

On his way down, the only sound to keep the teen company is the thumping of his heart, which accelerates by the second. Caleb stares down at the book wedged inside his pants. After what feels like an eternity, the elevator's metal door springs open.

The teen steps outside and immediately spots movement up the shadowy corridor. Karnitu throws the President over his shoulder with ease as he glides further away, grunting in annoyance with every step. Caleb sprints down the hall after them.

"Commander, stop! Let him go!" Caleb shouts, but the vile commander ignores the teen's plea. Karnitu reaches the end of the lengthy fourth floor corridor and peers over the balcony, staring deep into the soul of the Library. His fleet of Akache warriors wait in suspense down below, expecting their repulsive leader to reemerge victorious — with the Fura Mukedu. Karnitu decides to leap over the balcony, descending like a magnificent creature as he floats through the air, with the President draped over his shoulder. Caleb's Nikes skid to a stop as he watches the two plummet downward.

The teen has not a second to lose. He breaks into a mad dash, racing down the spiral staircase. Moments later, his soles land at the bottom. Exhausted, Caleb hunches over, his hands cradling his knees as he struggles to catch his breath.

Karnitu lifts President Reid into the air and slams him toward the center of room, allowing all to bear witness to the powerful creature's retribution.

"Aca cua the Fura Mukedu?" the commander barks one last time.

"I don't have the Fura Mukedu," President Reid says, spewing a mouthful of blood. He sits in a mangled ball, every inch of his body desperately pleading for a means to an end. Meanwhile, the First Lady is being forced to watch the horror of her husband's beating unfold, held back by two Akache warriors. Over the course of the last hour, she's made peace with her imminent fate, clenching onto the cross that hangs around her neck.

Karnitu walks over to face the First Lady, grabbing a fistful of her blonde hair. The perverse commander relentlessly boots President Reid in the chest. Each wallop prompts droplets of blood to trickle from his mouth.

"Stop it! You are killing him," the First Lady screams. Micky and Jaylen step back slowly, inching toward the corner, trying to go unnoticed. Karnitu spins out into a manic rage, hurling the First Lady's body thirty feet into the air. Her frail body delicately twirls, as though performing a ballet in midair — before she begins free falling toward the ground. The commander reveals a calculated grin, clearly pleased with the maiming to follow.

As the First Lady plummets downward, Karnitu hoists his spear into the sky. The sharp object connects with the woman's flesh, slicing right through, leaving her limp body skewered like nothing more than a piece of meat. Karnitu proudly holds up his trophy, puffing up his chest with a satisfied inhale. He detects the feeling of immense despair pulsing through the room before anyone lets out a word. The commander sets down the skewered First Lady, resting his foot onto her neck as he roughly pulls the spear loose from her decimated flesh.

"NOOO!" President Reid releases a cry of rage that nearly shakes the room. He pounds his fists into the floor until his hands throb. "Why?! You killed her! Monster!!" The President has officially been defeated. He relinquishes his fight to the universe, lying flat on the cold, hard floor, staring up into the massive crystal chandelier suspended above his head.

As the President digests the goings-on, his mind drifts to somewhere far, far away — the only solace he can cling to for the moment. Over and over again, his mind rehashes what else he could have said, what else he could have done to save his wife's life, or even exchange hers for his, but nothing sticks. Nothing he could have done would have saved her, and he knows it, but that's something he'll never be able to accept.

Caleb steps down from the staircase, staring in mournful disbelief. He carries himself toward the action, his eyes never leaving Karnitu.

"You have no right to our civilization."

"Aca cua the Fura Mukedu?" the commander annoyingly repeats, unaffected by the murder he just committed. He eyes the Book of Diop tucked in Caleb's pants. "Kahleo, aca cua the Fura Mukedu??" Karnitu screeches with a loud bark.

"Here. You want it, you can have it," Caleb snaps, flinging the book with all his force at the commander's feet. The teen can barely stand to look at the beastly creature any longer. Karnitu reaches down and roughly scoops up the book. Summoning every last scrap of his might, the great commander tries opening the historic document — but still, it will not budge.

The shrewd leader peers around the room, glaring at everyone watching as this ancient book mocks him and his vengeful obsession with it. Suddenly, the commander plucks Jaylen from his poor hiding spot within the shadows, instantly clutching the teen's throat. Karnitu's intimidating gaze lands on Caleb. The panicked teen backs away slowly. It tears him up inside, having to watch his friend become a surrogate for the evil commander, helplessly forced to spew the brutal pronouncements.

"You're weak – which is why the Palecians' dominion will remain all of your years."

"You'll be sorry if you harm him!" Caleb threatens.

"Kahleo, you must relinquish ties with your oppressor and commence to settling into your kingdom."

"Why should I believe you? You've killed loads of our people."

"How dare you insinuate that Akache is the cause of your demise. I am your eyes into the Palecians' souls. The question you should be asking yourself is who you would be without them."

"Over the last few days, I've tried seeing your skewed point of view. One thing remains… You are not the gateway to our freedom. My father once told me that adversity is a privilege," Caleb asserts. The confidence underlining his words throws Karnitu off-kilter for a moment. He grips Jaylen's throat tighter, restricting airflow. The following words come out of Jaylen's mouth in a deeper, more strained tone.

“The poor and weak conjure explanations, theories, conspiracies as a means of accepting mediocrity. I am here to create a harmonious experience for the Belivian species that is void of persecution!”

“You are a fucking liar!” Caleb screams at the top of his lungs. Indelible rage pumps through the teen’s soul, raw emotion guiding his unmitigated fury. His mind races, revisiting every last scene that’s gone on through the nightmare brought upon this world by the unbearable alien invader. “Enough! Let us live!”

“That’s exactly what I’m here to do, Kahleo,” the commander calmly states. All of a sudden, the ancient book resting at Karnitu’s feet gently vibrates, rising a few inches off the floor. It begins twirling for a few moments before settling back down to the ground — near Caleb. Karnitu squints down at the book, then upward to the uneasy teen once more.

“I’ve overstepped my assumptions, Kahleo. Writing you off as ‘weak’ could have been the bane of our existence.”

“If you want a fight, I’ll give you one,” Caleb assures. Karnitu locks eyes with the mocha-skinned freshman.

“Open the book,” the commander demands.

"I can't!"

"Kahleo, your distinct emotions is the pathway to the truth."

"I don't know what you are talking about," Caleb insists. The commander takes a moment to peer upward at the glistening chandelier hanging overhead, searching for the proper response. Clearly thinking unhappy thoughts, Karnitu squeezes Jaylen's neck even tighter, strangling what little life remains from the flailing teen's lanky body.

"Open the book!"

"I don't know how!" Caleb notices as his friend quickly loses oxygen. His eyes slip shut. Jaylen's body settles into an immobile shock, his vigorous movements coming to a close. "Please, stop it! You're going to kill him. He's Belivian!"

"Oh, he's Belivian now?" Karnitu mocks, refusing to let up on the teen's scrawny neck. His razor-sharp fangs protrude as he smiles with glee, taunting Caleb with a sadistic cackle. The lengthy red ponytail sprouting from the tip of his skull whirls about in a frenzied mess.

Making an unexpected return, the chilling red mist of the Akache flows through the room, like a tornado ravaging a rundown trailer park, leaving nothing behind but dirt and dust. Warriors repeatedly slam down the tip of their spears against the floor, orchestrating a hypnotic melody. The mysteriously eerie tune of the Akache fills the halls of the Library.

Caleb tries to take a step forward, hoping to save his friend, but he's unable to move from his current position, his legs suddenly immobile. The heartbroken teen watches as the life force drains from his best friend's body, and there is absolutely nothing he can do about it. Something that Caleb's father once said to him begins ringing in his ears; the words are deliberate and precise. You have a purpose, Caleb. Always follow your purpose. The thoughtful quote of his father spurs him into action. Refusing to give up, Caleb retrieves the book from the ground, cradling it in his palms as one would a newborn baby.

"Please open," Caleb whispers, desperation apparent in his voice. Nothing happens. Nevertheless, he tries again. "I need to save my friend, please open." The words uttered come out in a hoarse tone, uncertainty at the helm. The ancient black book remains closed, staring back, taunting the teen. As tears well up in Caleb's eyes, a certain calmness envelops him. His signature confidence begins to resurface. A strong tingling sensation caresses his chest, tickling down deep within his soul. Caleb meditates, his mind turning back to Jaylen's deadly descent from the Akache mothership just a few days prior.

"Wait a minute," Caleb says, his internal convictions soaring, "freedom comes with choice." The teen finds his way back to his strength. Settling his deep brown eyes back onto the book, he releases a sweet whisper in the most tranquil tone. "My choice. I am choosing to open this book."

Miraculously, the book springs open. The Akache warriors' eccentric chants swirling through the room settle into a collective hush. Out of the book ignites a blinding glow that settles into a mesmerizing hum of illumination. Caleb frantically thumbs through the pages, searching for the unknown – but this book is one void of words. The pages are completely empty.

"That's weird. Why would they secure an empty book?" Caleb asks curiously. Jaylen's body hits the floor with a resounding thump as Karnitu releases him from his clutches. Micky runs over to help the fallen teen, dragging him away to safety among the shadows. The commander stomps over to Caleb, snatching the book right out of his hands. He scours the pages vigorously and comes to the same conclusion. Karnitu attempts to tear the book in half but every inch of it seems impenetrable, despite his superhuman strength. The commander's intense gaze now shifts to the door. An intruding wind comes barreling through, leveling the double doors. Enchanting white light explodes through the entryway, temporarily blinding Caleb. Lingering within the blistering illumination is the majestic outline of the Akache warriors. Leading the pack, marching right in Caleb's direction – the mighty Akache warrior, Bree. She's flanked by a fleet of Akache warriors, all of whom are quite larger in size than the average Akache. Loose-fitting garments drape her devastatingly beautiful exterior. Indistinguishable writings coat the feminine warrior's robust shell, each nearly impossible to decipher. The long red ponytail occupying her head wraps suggestively around her neck, covering her perfectly curvaceous breasts. A minimal piece of fabric hangs from her slender waist, landing right above her knees, proudly displaying the prominent muscles in her legs. The warrior's aura moves through the door before she does, instantly melting Caleb's heart. Within his mind, the teen is transported to the bridge a few miles away from the Genesee Mall. That same bridge is where the two first met. Caleb's posture shifts as a flood of emotion races through his body.

"Bree," Caleb calls out. "You're back." He can't help but smile up at her. The stunning Akache warrior stays puts, waiting for the teen to approach. "Bree, it's me, Caleb." She keeps a watchful eye set on him, much like a cat stalking its prey. Caleb steps closer still. "Bree, are you in there?" The warrior looks down, noticing the black book clenched tightly in his hands. Caleb follows her eyes.

"Aca cua the Fura Mukedu?" the warrior asks with a seductive gaze. Caleb looks up, momentarily losing his breath as he realizes that her garments have been upgraded to provide the perfect fit to her athletic frame.

"I don't have it, Bree."

"Aca cua the Fura Mukedu?" she asks again. Caleb gingerly takes another step closer. The mocha-skinned teen admires Bree's immaculate exterior. He gets lost in thought for several moments, studying the ravishing female warrior standing before him. All of a sudden, the Akache dialect of her speech fades away. She settles into her old self and begins to communicate in English.

"Give us the Fura Mukedu, Caleb."

"Bree. He's using you!" Caleb shouts, glancing backward at Karnitu. The commander waits patiently, watching the scene play out with a curious eye. Caleb continues. "Bree, this was never about helping us. He wants to destroy us. I feel it."

"No, Caleb, he wants to set us free. It's the only way."

"He's lying," Caleb counters. The warrior's vocal inflections increasingly become emotionless, more direct.

"Where is the Fura Mukedu, Caleb?" she demands. The teen looks the female warrior up and down, starting with her smug smile. He searches deeply for the girl he's loved from the very beginning. Slowly, he makes peace within himself that she may be gone forever.

"I know what he wants with the Fura Mukedu, Bree. It's not what you think." This statement sends the warrior over the edge. Her animal-like instincts quickly take over. She leaps through the air, twisting with great power, before striking the curious teen with a crippling kick to the chest. The force of Caleb's body topples three bookshelves before crashing into the gigantic portrait of Thomas Jefferson that's been mounted to the wall for decades. Lying in a heap, the bruised teen pushes off the painting, stumbling for a moment before regaining his footing.

"Bree, stop," Caleb says in surrender. "It's me— " As Caleb takes a step forward, Bree lunges into the air, rotating with extreme precision, wrapping both legs tightly around the teen's neck. She reverses her strength in place, doing a backflip, sending Caleb crashing through the doors leading to the foyer of the building. He does a nosedive, his body skidding to a bumpy stop. Karnitu watches from the sidelines, reveling in the exhibition, rooting on the one-sided battle. Caleb's mangled body lies sprawled out across the foyer's marble floor, his shirt partially ripped away from his body.

Meanwhile, the grim battle has provided Micky and Jaylen the opportunity to slip away, darting up the winding staircase. The two hobble to safety. They watch from the second floor, hiding just below the balcony.

All eyes widen as suddenly the ancient 5-inch by 7-inch book lifts from the floor, boomeranging itself through the doors, into the foyer, and finally, landing at Caleb's feet. Sauntering over, Karnitu jams his size sixteen foot into Caleb's scrawny neck, restricting his movements.

"Aca cua the Fura Mukedu?" the commander barks at a high decibel, shattering the wealth of historic statues on display throughout the vicinity. The book itself comes to life… It snakes its way from the floor, onto Caleb's back. The intricate markings embedded within his flesh begins to glow, appearing legible for the first time. Bold, colorful lines trace a gentle trail on his skin, leading from his back, to the book.

The historical document opens on its own accord. Vivid markings similar to those one would find in an old-time map gradually appear, filling every page of the book.

Spying from overhead, Micky whispers to Jaylen, revealing her inner thoughts. "Look, Jaylen. I knew it. The designs on his back are the map."

"What map?" Jaylen whispers back, confused.

"The map that leads them to the Fura Mukedu," Micky clarifies. Still feeling quite drained from Karnitu's near suffocation tactic, Jaylen gently pulls his phone from his pocket, wincing as he does so. He takes a much-needed moment to himself and then proceeds to do something he should have done hours ago. Holding his phone up to his mouth, he whispers.

"Caneala, what is the Fura Mukedu?"

From the phone, a robotic woman's voice responds. "The Fura Mukedu is a worldly indoctrinated myth created by the Egyptians during 3200 B.C."

"Tell us more about the Fura Mukedu," Jaylen prods.

Again, the robotic woman's voice answers. "The Egyptians used the Fura Mukedu to help ward off sinister civilizations opting to take over its land." The loud explanations draw attention from down below, prompting glances from the Akache warriors. Micky and Jaylen manage to go unnoticed for the time being.

"Shhh, turn that thing off, Jaylen. You'll get us killed," Micky screeches, snatching the phone right out of the teen's hands, turning it off.

Down below, Caleb still lies unmoving on the floor. The book glides along his skin, eventually settling on his naked back. Three distinguished designs resembling ancient monuments rest on various parts of his back. Each of these markings create paths to the elevated book. The ancient monuments represent three of the four disciples of Diop. The obscure symbols radiate, peeling away from Caleb's chocolate skin, hovering inches over the teen's body.

"Oh my God! That map points to the Fura Mukedu," Micky says.

"So, what's the fucking point of the book?" Jaylen asks.

"Don't you get it? When all four books have been unlocked, it provides the exact coordinates to where the Fura Mukedu may be kept. The commander has the first three." Micky peeks from the balcony, watching intently.

All of a sudden, the presumed fourth disciple of Diop magically appears across the book's pages. Karnitu squints, his eyes surveying the exact coordinates of the Fura Mukedu. A deceitful grin snakes its way across the commander's face. He points to the door, prompting his entire fleet, including Bree, to file into the streets in preparation for their journey. The moment the warriors deploy, Micky and Jaylen sprint down the spiral stairs, joining their friend. As they approach, the book settles, dropping to the floor. Caleb sits up groggily as if awakening from a nap.

"This is getting ridiculous," Caleb starts. "How long was I out?"

"Are you okay?" Jaylen asks, giving his friend the once-over.

"Yes, I'm okay. My molecular structure is allowing me to regenerate more quickly."

"Yeah, you're beginning to move and act like they do," Micky says in agreement.

"Caleb, I think they are headed to the fourth point." With that, Caleb rises to his feet, his strong teenage voice filling the foyer, bouncing off the walls.

"We've got to stop them." Caleb begins walking to do the door. Jaylen and Micky lag behind. They shoot each other a look of confusion.

"And how are we supposed to do that, Cal?" Jaylen inquires.

"I'll know when I get there." Jaylen chases after Caleb, who's almost to the door by now.

"Cal, you are not being rational. We survived these fuckers. Let's lie low for a minute."

"If you knew what I knew, Jaylen, you wouldn't have proposed such an awful idea," Caleb states ominously. Jaylen throws his hands up in the air, waiting for an explanation that doesn't come as fast as he would like. He watches as Caleb reaches for the door, his palm turning the knob.

Micky contemplates what to say but harsh words escape her mouth before she can suck them back in. "You want to kill like they do."

Micky's sobering words shake Caleb to the core. He pivots, turning on his heels to face both of his friends. "It is not my doing, but I'll fight this thing inside of me."

"Caleb, I think you know that it's a losing battle." Despite her condescending tone, Caleb allows her to finish. "Man up. Tell us what this Fura Mukedu really is about." Just then, the already dim lighting within the room flickers, signaling the presence of an otherworldly entity.

Caleb approaches Micky and Jaylen. "It took me a while to understand. For the past few days, I've tried every remedy to fight the urges and temptation to align with Karnitu. But something kept strengthening me, guiding me away long enough to balance my demons." Jaylen and Micky each hold their breath, listening intently, watching their friend's animated movements as he attempts to explain himself. "Karnitu wants to destroy the universe and create another one."

"That's fucking impossible! How do you know this?" Jaylen asks, rubbing the back of his head.

"I told you a few days ago, Jaylen. He and I are one and the same."

Micky stares Caleb square in the face. "What is the Fura Mukedu?" A soft hum sounds from above, its rhythm one of calm.

The soothing tone relaxes Caleb, giving him the strength to go on with his story. He points to the sky with the tip of his index finger. "That's the Fura Mukedu. It clothes you, feeds you, and will warn you when appropriate. It is the life force of the universe that no one knows but everyone understands. I never thought it was possible to believe in this stuff. But I am 100-percent sure now that it wasn't Akache who visited me that fateful day. It was the Fura Mukedu, warning me – us – about what was to come."

Caleb turns his back to his friends, admiring the Akache designs wrapped around his arms before continuing. "The Fura Mukedu has been hidden away for billions of years. A host of civilizations have tried to find it but have repeatedly failed. Karnitu used us in his wicked games to find it."

"Wait. So, why take us along on his deceitful ride into the abyss?" Jaylen asks with a confused look on his face.

"Scientists have found that African American DNA is presumably indestructible. Our strength is impenetrable, laced with the stuff that creates worlds. For centuries, we alone have created races and alternate species all around the universe, unbeknownst to us. Karnitu knew that if he had a chance against the Fura Mukedo, he had to first reinforce his army. And now, he's using us like pawns to capture the greatest relic known to the universe."

Caleb walks back over to the door. His final words hang in the air, daunting, lingering like a rich, black smoke that chokes you on impact. "The Fura Mukedu created all that is, and all that will be. She—" Caleb notices that his two friends are frozen in place. Jaylen tries moving, but the shock doesn't allow him to do so.

"Yes," Caleb continues, "the Fura Mukedu is the creator of the universe, the heartbeat of every civilization out of the naked universe. It's quite difficult to quantify but undoubtedly true. Her darkened melanin is what powers her ruthless nature, like a black hole, destroying all that obstructs its path."

Micky turns to Jaylen, who takes a few curious steps forward, a look of proud shock radiating from his face. "So, the creator of the universe is a Black woman? The Fura Mukedu is a Black woman! I knew it," Jaylen quietly crows to himself.

Caleb continues. "It is the Fura Mukedu that has brought illness to my doorstep purposely. She knew this moment would come, and she wanted to warn us. Karnitu has conjured his army to kill her. She is ALIVE —

hidden deep beneath the Earth's crust, and if they find her…"

With that, Caleb stops, withholding the most crucial assessment of his declaration. He knows that speaking any further would spur a barrage of unwanted questions, so the teen keeps mum, silently trekking for the door. Micky tries for the last time to illicit more information from her trance-induced friend.

"Caleb, stop," Micky says, desperation in her voice. "What are we missing?" Jaylen takes his chance, attempting to run after Caleb.

Without looking back, Caleb mirrors Karnitu's intricate movements. Gently squeezing his hand into a clenched fist, the gesture immediately halts Jaylen's movement in mid-sprint, the teen's legs paralyzed in place.

"I can't move my legs, bro," Jaylen screeches. On a mission, Caleb explodes through the double doors, exiting the library.

"Oh my God," Micky squeals in a low hush. Her whisper peppered in angst tickles at Jaylen's eardrums. "Our friend is gone."

"What are you saying?" Jaylen inquires.

"He's no longer Caleb. It's his destiny to become one of them. If he finds the Fura Mukedu first, he's strong enough to kill her… Then us."

"You're crazy!" Jaylen spews, while trying his hardest to shake away the numbness in his legs. Now alone, Micky and Jaylen linger in the center of the foyer, the weight of the world falling strictly on their teenage shoulders. They remain motionless, helplessly watching as the red mist slowly returns, encapsulating the outside of the Library of Congress.

"It's starting," Micky says. "All we can do now is pray…"

Made in the USA
Columbia, SC
02 July 2021